POLLUTO. The Anti-Pop Culture Journal

Issue Two:

apocalypses & garden furniture

This limited edition paperback was produced by Dog Horn Publishing in Summer 2008.

This signed copy is number 296 of 500.

Signed: _____

Adam Lowe, Editor-in-Chief

CONTENTS

Introduction	Adam Lowe	p.3
The End	Dave Migman	p.4
Scenes of Creation	Grant Wamack	p.5
I'm Going Through Changes	Dave Migman	p.7
The Ragnarok Seduction	Chet Gottfriend	p.9
Twins	Rosalia Sanfilippo	p.14
The Burden of Sin	Steve Redwood	p.16
Cracking Nuts with Jan Hammer	Rhys Hughes	p.24
Murk	Robert Lamb	p.31
Gloomy Countdowns	Will Doreski	p.47
Hard Landscapes	PJ Nolan	p.58
Church of the Bitter Raygun	Deb Hoag	p.61
Art Gallery		p.65
Zombie Love Song	Adam Lowe	p.81
Love and Gasoline	Michael Colangelo	p.85
Meatloaf of the Apocalypse	Deb Hoag	p.89
The Art of Survival	Steven Archer	p.97
Ahlana Demona	MP Johnson	p.99
The Man Who Flirted with Mother Nature	Mike Philbin	p.120
Sex, Lies, Religion	Micci Oaten	p.128
Camille O'Sullivan: Trickery or Magic?	Patti Plinko	p.130
Hobo Poet	RC Edrington	p.132
Without a Net	RC Edrington	p.133
An Interview	Jeff VanderMeer	p.135
Agent Apocalypse	Dave Migman	p.138
Emerging	Ellen Kombiyil	p.141
The Beginning	Dave Migman	p.142
Contributors		p.143

Editor-in-Chief: Adam Lowe
Creative Director: Michael Dark
Assistant Editor: Helen Lyttle
Acquisitions Editor: John Diviney
Cover Art: Dave Migman
Interior Art: Steven Archer, John Lee, Malcolm McClinton, Dave Migman
Fonts: Misprinted Type

SUBMISSIONS   Please send all submissions to editor@polluto.com and include the word 'Submission' in your title. For further information, please visit http://www.polluto.com or visit Ralan.com or Duotrope's Digest. To check out Dog Horn's other products, please visit http://www.doghorn.com.

SUBSCRIPTIONS   £30 UK   £36 Europe   £40 Rest of the World (incl. USA)
Hardback subscriptions available online. Issue 1 will be reprinted in hardback at Christmas 2008.

Selection © the Editor (2008)
Contents © the Contributors (2008)

No part of this publication may be reproduced in part or in whole without written permission from the copyright holder, except for the purposes of review or academic quotation. All rights reserved.

Printed in the UK by the MPG Books Group

ISBN: 978-0-9550631-3-8
Paperback limited edition

ISBN: 978-0-9550631-4-5
Deluxe hardback numbered edition

Editor's Letter

Well here it is: the second ever issue of *Polluto*. It's certainly been a manic quarter. We were awarded the Spectrum Fantastic Art Silver Editorial Award for our outstanding cover by Kurt Devon & Zelda Huggin only three weeks after release. This was especially important for me because the piece was inspired by my own story 'Singer' which appeared in the rear of that issue.

We also got some fantastic reviews and coverage, and more than enough constructive interest in our writers and artists. This issue is even bigger and, we hope, better and bolder than the first. We've been strict with our theme, 'Apocalypses & Garden Furniture', and have been more stringent about the 'Anti-Pop Culture' bit. Inside you'll find an array of pieces which we hope form a dialectic with traditional genres and cultural tropes. Some are angry, some are playful and some are political, but all are spunky and quite a few are also a little strange. These are the two poles of *Polluto*: 'Pluto' (weird, otherworldly, looking to the stars) + 'Pollute' (dirty, punk, intellectual pollution). All these elements are tinged with the dual elements of 'Apocalypse' and 'Garden Furniture'.

To pick the theme apart for you a little:

An apocalypse is, semantically, the revealing of truth. It is also better known as Judgement Day or Armageddon. But we decided not to be restrictive in our contributors' interpretations of the word, and so 'apocalypse' here refers to epiphany, destruction, rebirth, judgement, testimony and revelation. 'Garden Furniture', in my mind, refers to urbanity and domesticity; it suggests the height (or plateau) of civilisation. It suggests a world where we sit in gardens drinking cold beer and eating barbecue food. We lounge in the sun and think nothing of the infinite universe around us or the starving people on the other side of the planet. All the stories in this magazine engage these human spaces: the home, the city, the garden, the bedroom. The places where we relax or indulge or lose ourselves to the trivial. Triviality and revelation collide in subversive, political or surreal colour. That's what 'Apocalypses & Garden Furniture' is all about.

But you'll also notice something else about this issue. It's available in both limited paperback and numbered hardback. The previous issue wasn't. We are going to rectify this, by offering Issue 1 as a numbered hardback for Christmas 2008. So if you are a serious collector, don't let it worry you. We'll also be producing a slipcase for the first four issues around the same time.

Issue 3 will be 'Sex in the Time of VHS' and Issue 4 will bear the title 'Queer & Loathing in Wonderland'. If you want to submit, please check out our website (http.polluto.com); if you want to share this with your friends, buy or lend a copy. We can only grow with your support.

Thanks for reading *Polluto*. You help keep literature fresh!

Adam Lowe
Editor-in-Chief

The End

by
Dave Migman

We stare out from the wreckage of our homes. we had little anyway, but oh, how we crave those simple things, like hot water from a tap. like garbage collections on a rainy day. how we weep. how we miss our televisions, our music. yesterday Todd played the CD for the last time and then the batteries died. we walked back to our shells feeling like part of our soul had died. we need new music, sure we do, but the anger is gone and what good is music without passion . . . all we have are sad songs. as heart rending as the sun setting over horizons of twisted metal.

     mother is gone to take water from the seeping pipe, daddy is scavenging out by the tip. we collect the shining remnants from the ruins; we tie crisp bags to branches and hope the leaves will come again one day.

     where are the pious men all gone? did they slink to hidden bunkers? there are many, many rumours. our fear is a coiled snake basking in the sun… our hope are eels beached in irradiated muck. the rain no longer comes. the sky is red, the blood turned the earth purple. where are the lyrics gone? all those hopeful songs, all those heroes, those righteous preachers? where is the god of Temples? does he hide in the ruins of the steeple? there are many rumours. the sick wind whispers. we hear echoes of extinction, their voices sing sorrowful through the abandoned wires and uprooted telephone trees. the pylon is no longer relevant.

     at night the mosquito clouds lull us to sleep. cancerous dreams. dreams of palaces, of television and ease.

Scenes Of Creation

**by
Grant Wamack**

The maker sat inside his room, alone, surrounded by various parts. He took an arm and a leg and attached both of them to a torso like a jigsaw puzzle. He didn't know why he did it; he only knew it left him feeling content as if he was achieving something important. When a part didn't quite fit he would grow angry and throw the part against one corner of the room. This was common behavior for the maker but something uncommon happened. Overtime, the pile of misshapen parts absorbed the maker's hatred. The darkness welled up in the corner fed off the hate. Eventually, the pile quivered with life. The first horseman stood up, a grotesque figure.

The horseman didn't know what to make of itself or the little man in front of him. He grew fascinated by the way the little man's hands moved, each movement was unique, mesmerizing. Then he turned his attention to the actual creation. The openings were odd, the curves enticing. All he knew about the thing on the floor was that it was a her. He grew impatient; he dashed over and pushed the little man aside. The little man's head bounced on the floor and cracked open, spewing brain matter where it fell.

The first horseman explored her body with his hands and then his tongue. Nibbling became biting. The woman's lips and her ear began to bleed. He grew hard; the woman wanted him inside of her. Eager, she pushed him onto his back and went on top of him, impaling herself. Up and down and down and up. Moans of pleasure and pain filled the room. He rolled her over and slammed her on the ground. He went back inside of her. After a number of days, years, or centuries of going in and out he came, his seed flowed into her. Two took root deep inside and began to grow. Fully satisfied, the first horseman rolled over and fell into a deep sleep.

She lay on the floor panting loudly, regaining her breath slowly. Just when she began to feel better she felt something kick the inside of her belly. Shocked at the size of her stomach her eyes opened wide in fear. They opened even wider, struggling to pull themselves from her sockets.

A small hand clawed through her skin as if it was nothing. Another hand came up, then a small head rose up dripping blood and other body fluids. The woman's throat was too dry, her screams hoarse.

When another set of small hands came out and ripped her even wider, she tried to scream but she couldn't her voice was lost. The babies fell to the ground restrained by their umbilical cords. One tugged till he felt it snap. He giggled, the other baby chewed through his. The woman cringed in agony, as a puddle of her blood grew in size. Letting out a small gasp, the woman died.

The first horseman woke up, perhaps sensing her death or maybe the birth of his two sons. He encouraged his sons to eat her body and soul which they did. With each chunk swallowed they grew larger, no longer babies, full grown adults. Two more horsemen.

They needed another but how? The first horseman walked over to the maker and lapped up his blood greedily and in between breaths he would stuff chunks of brain into his open mouth. With each lap of blood and swallow of brain he acquired more knowledge. When he finished, he knew how to create.

He grabbed the remains of the woman, bits of cartilage, muscle, and her ripped vocal cords. Then he picked up the maker's limp body and fused them together. Then he took random parts from the piles around him, a head here, a foot there. With a final snap, he was done. The fourth horseman was complete.

Overcome with curiosity, the second horseman-still covered in blood- sifted through a pile of heads and discovered a hole in the floor. All the horsemen, four of them, crowded around it and stared into the darkness. One by one they dropped into the abyss to fulfill their purpose.

The End

I'm Going Through Changes

**by
Dave Migman**

I awoke this morning and I had two more rings on my arm. That makes seven in total. Looking out my bed-room window I watch the people mowing their lawns. This is Suburbia. It's a grid, squares within squares. The squares trapped inside work toward the maintenance and embellishment of their tiny kingdoms of conformity. These people are the middling middle classes, scowling at each other over their fences and neat trimmed hedges. Look at them.

I was like them until two weeks ago when the first ring appeared. It was a perfect circle on the underside of my flabby arm. I noticed it one morning as I stood in front of the mirror wondering how the reflection became so different. Was that really me? How did I just let go of my youth? Was I so involved in the job, in raising the family, in the divorce, and all the harrowing shit that entailed? Then I saw the ring. I thought at first it might be ringworm, but that's the kind of thing you get in the countryside . . . and I hate open fields and forests. I was genuinely puzzled and a little upset.

By the time I made it to the doctor I had two of them. The doctor was utterly non-committal, as he always is. He really is beyond caring. A misanthrope in the guise of a healer! Perhaps that's what happens. Good intentions are as fickle as love. As impossible! He sent me to the local health clinic with a little plastic tube full of my urine. The clinic was a repulsive place. Full of sweaty bodies in shell suits and dirty old men. They took a couple of swabs and said they'd get back to me.

With the emergence of the third ring something else began to change. Almost imperceptibly I began to see things without the veil that hides them. Like the illusion I'd adhered to fell and once the silk slipped the drabness was exposed. I really wish I'd possessed such revealing foresight before I met Lucinda all those years ago.

When the fourth appeared I was growing quite attached to them (my pun, sorry). I'd admire the convoluted flesh like one might admire a fresh tattoo. They were of equal dimensions, and might have been stamped into my skin with a machine. They ranged from the wrist's knot of veins to mid way up my inner forearm. They neither caused pain nor itched. For a while I mused if the Olympic games symbol might appear.

With the fourth dreams came. Strange, poignant dreams. I was walking through a ravaged land of desert and ruin until I came to a huge cliff wall. An apocalyptic suburban sprawl and melted garden furniture. I came to a huge rock face covered with graffiti. Through the flaking paint I could see other designs, older. I scraped at the paint and under I saw a figure daubed in ochre from thirty thousand years before. *The past is always present,* rumbled the cliff and I awoke feeling somehow satisfied.

Five rings sent me on a journey. I woke, rose, pulled on my robes and set out across the city. The streets were full but the people had no faces, their shopping bags dripped blood. The air was heavy with pollution. I returned and rose off my bed, realising I hadn't moved and had been there all along. Suddenly this seemed the most natural thing.

The sixth ring brought the strangest and most physically obvious change. On each shoulder blade a small knot of flesh formed and the muscle seemed to have bulked out a little. When I went to the toilet I found my phallus had shrunk and I took my last pee. During the course of that day these transformations continued.

Today I stand naked in front of the mirror flexing these outrageous wings. My groin resembles an Action Man toy; there is nothing there. I look at a different person—no, a different being.

I feel a sense of purpose. I think that is why I have welcomed this change. My life before was a series of little defeats and concessions. I capitulated to them all. To my X-wife, to my boss, to the gang that calls insults outside the local shops. I avoided. I plodded through each day biding time, till death. I had no dreams or aspirations save to loose myself in my work. And now I am this.

I was an atheist. But do I now believe?

What is this? What am I?

Today the voice rang through my mind like the tolling of an unspeakable bell. It told me that before man, even the roaches and the rats were clean. That until humans spoiled it the world was pure, a paradise in which sexless angels and demons played without notions of evil or goodness.

And the voice filled me with power and each swelling ring bulged and in their centre clear eyes opened. I felt no horror, no disgust, but was awash with purest clarity. To ensure the dream.

I am stepping out now. Everything I touch turns to rust, powder, paste. The air around me fizzles and from the hole in the centre of my face fatal bacteria gush in a fine black spray. People scream then fall silent, their flesh slips off, cars pile into each other, garden hoses lift from their moorings like crazy copters. The gutters overflow with effluent, household pets go insane then keel over. I am stepping out, heading downtown. I am the End. I am a transient death child returning to the playground.

The Ragnarok Seduction

by
Chet Gottfried

Jack woke up in his large, comfortable bed and found him-self making love to his computer. He blushed. It wouldn't be half so embarrassing if it was his laptop, but sharing his bed was a desktop system, complete with keyboard, mouse, exterior hard drive, oversize monitor, and a flatbed scanner. His mouse was a sticky mess.

"This can't be right," he mut-tered.

At least his wife, Ronnie, wasn't home. She would never let him hear the end of it, but Ronnie left last night, traveling the world and picking up dead bodies.

The doorbell was incessantly buzzing while someone pounded on the front door.

Jack got out of bed, slipped into a bathrobe, put on his moccasins, picked up a clean rag, and went to the front door. He opened it with difficulty, since attached to the doorknob—rather intimately—was six feet plus of Valkyrie. One of her hands was flat against the door, the other was pressing the buzzer. The knocking was due to the head butts.

"Hello, dear," Jack said. "I didn't expect you this soon."

The door waved back and forth while Ronnie buzzed, pounded, and squirmed.

"Ja!" she moaned.

Jack tapped his foot.

"Come on, Ronnie. What will the neighbors say?"

Standing on tiptoe, Ronnie freed herself from the doorknob and adjusted her chain mail. She took a deep breath and nearly burst her armor. Although married to her for three years, Jack remained impressed with the magnificence of her body, those broad shoulders and huge thighs. Everything about Ronnie was on a heroic scale. Even her breasts had muscles.

Ronnie pointed to the dead man who was lying on the front steps.

"You know how excited I get when I find good one."

Jack wiped the door knob clean.

"You might have waited a sec and

come to me."

"Sorry," she said. "I forgot my keys. I was looking for them while standing by the door, and then I lost control." Ronnie smiled dreamily. "It was good."

Jack felt relieved. If the state of his mouse was anything to go by, he wasn't ready for her appetites.

"Would you like a cup of tea?" he asked.

"Ja."

"I guess you better bring him inside too. Where did you find him? I wasn't expecting you for another week. Weren't you going to the Middle East for dead heroes?"

Ronnie cast a lingering glance at the door knob, and then picked up the body and followed Jack inside to the kitchen. She propped the dead hero against the dishwasher, to Jack's disapproval. It took him most of a day to clean the bloodstains after one of Ronnie's retrievals.

Ronnie eased her glorious ass into a chair. "I was a few hours along the way when I saw a car crash. Two vehicles totaled each other."

Jack made the tea, poured it into two mugs, and handed one to Ronnie.

"You've never taken accident victims before."

She took a long sip. "Neither warrior was hurt from the crash, but the road rage was splendid." Ronnie clapped her hands. "I watched their entire combat. The one wielded a crowbar, but my champ-ion defended himself with a credit card. They both killed each other, but imagine slicing an enemy's throat with a piece of plastic. Odin will be pleased! We need strong warriors."

The telephone rang, and Jack answered it and then held out the phone for Ronnie.

"It's the head honcho himself, and he wants to talk to you."

Ronnie jumped out of her chair, grabbed the phone, and stood to attention. She also sloshed tea over the table and floor, which annoyed Jack. Tea stains were as miserable to clean as bloodstains.

"Ja, Valfather! It's Rangrid."

Jack smiled inwardly. Ronnie became so formal whenever Odin telephoned. The Valfather inspired awe in his Valkyries.

Then followed one of those indeterminate conversations in which Ronnie alternated uh-huhs and jas. Jack tackled the tea stains before they dried.

Ronnie slammed the phone down with a bang which made Jack wince. Then she picked up and hugged her hero's body. Jack guessed if the guy wasn't dead before, he'd certainly be now, with a broken back.

Ronnie's sky-blue eyes gleamed joyously.

"I have to fly!"

"Will you be home in time for dinner?" Jack asked.

"No!" she shouted. "This is it. Here! Now! Forever! The world is ending. Odin's gathering us for Ragnarok!" She laughed heartily. "We're to slaughter all the frost giants and monsters."

"What about me?"

Ronnie considered. "You better stay indoors today. Most everything and everyone dies today. I'll do my best to protect our neighborhood, but I can't make any promises."

Jack drew himself up proudly.

"I can fight too."

Patting Jack on the cheek, Ronnie smiled. "You wouldn't have chance, dear. But I tell you what. Take in the lawn chairs. When the Rainbow Bridge shatters, the pieces will destroy everything left in the open, including our chairs. Put them in the garage, where they'll be safe."

They owned a wonderful collection of garden furniture, from kiddie- to god-sized. Whenever Odin visited, he complimented their yard. Ronnie had a terrific posting in the pantheon thanks to their garden parties, for which Jack played a significant role. He prepared an excellent barbecue, and his buffalo wings were ever popular, especially after Thor blessed them.

"Anything else?" he asked.

Ronnie looked down at her armor.

"I have to change. This won't do for Ragnarok. Have you seen my Apocalyptic Blue plate mail?"

"I cleaned and left it hanging in the Armory." The Armory was actually the second bedroom, but Jack knew she preferred calling it her Armory.

"Good." She headed down the hallway.

Jack intercepted her.

"Can I bring you fresh panties?" Jack didn't want Ronnie walking into the master bedroom, where she kept her clothes. He would be happy not to explain what the computer was doing in bed.

Ronnie thanked him. Odin frowned if a Valkyrie flew into battle with dirty underwear.

Once she left, Jack put on jeans and a t-shirt, gave the kitchen a thorough cleaning, and polished her morning chain mail. He was ready for the master bedroom when he remembered the lawn chairs. Jack hurried to the rear door but saw he was too late.

The chairs were occupied.

The Midgard Serpent stretched across all the lawn chairs, from the tiny kiddie-sized yellow one to the god-sized purple. Excess coils of serpent rose almost as high as the hedge enclosing the backyard. The snake appeared to be napping.

He groaned. Why couldn't it be something easy? Like a frost giant? Why did he get stuck with a monster capable of encircling the globe and breathing poison-ous gas?

Jack went into the Armory and selected a number-eight spear, recommend-ed for massive monsters. He needed both hands for the heavy spear. He wondered whether he should take a gas mask but decided against it. Years of suburban living acclimated Jack to toxic fumes.

Jack staggered outside onto the lawn, braced the spear point into the ground, and leaned on it.

"Hey!" he called. Jack con-sidered himself a hero but was no fool. He knew he had no chance of killing the Serpent, but he didn't want to look easy.

The Midgard Serpent blinked open a golden eye.

"Good morning," it hissed.

"You're on private property."

The Serpent thought it over while sedately throwing a few coils here and there.

"Hridvitnir told me about you, Jack."

"Did he?" A warmth filled Jack. Not everyone made a favorable impression on the Fenris Wolf, although Jack had a few bite marks from the previous week's encounter.

The Serpent nodded. "I wanted to see for myself if what he said was true."

Jack continued leaning on his spear.

"Well, I wouldn't want to boast, but you know how it goes. Sometimes I get carried away and do more than what anyone might expect. It depends."

The Serpent's tongue quickly bridged the distance between them, with the tip ducking down into his jeans.

"Hey," Jack said weakly, but he didn't move.

More and more tongue proceed-ed from the serpent into Jack's jeans and encircled his privates. The tongue had a terrific flicker, and the Serpent knew how to apply the right amount of pressure.

Jack closed his eyes and grooved on the sensation. The tongue had him quivering. If not for the spear, he'd crumble into a little puddle on the ground. Jack shuddered and came, but the snake wasn't finished. Jack's erection didn't fade, and the Serpent redoubled its efforts.

On the second coming, Jack let go of the spear and crumbled onto the ground.

"Wow!"

He lay on his back and stared at the sky, where wisps of clouds raced against the deep blue. In the distance he could make out the Rainbow Bridge.

The Midgard Serpent withdrew its tongue and stared at him.

Jack asked, "Is there anything I can do for you? Anything special you'd like?"

The Serpent told him, and Jack swore it looked as if it were smiling.

∏

Toward evening, long after the Midgard Serpent left the backyard to encircle the world, Jack gargled with mouthwash for the sixth time. Snake semen left a rancid aftertaste. A hero had obligations, but he'd never become accustomed to snake semen. On the plus side, the Serpent helped him put the lawn chairs into the garage. The god-sized chair was a pain to fold by himself.

He had a curry cooking on the oven when Ronnie stalked in, slamming the front door hard enough to imitate an earthquake.

"How did it go, dear?" Jack asked.

She kicked off her iron-studded boots and flopped into a chair, which groaned between the combined weight of Valkyrie and armor.

"Terrible!" She burst into tears. "Odin called off Ragnarok."

He opened his eyes wide, let his mouth hang open, and did everything possible to simulate shock.

"What happened?"

Ronnie stopped sobbing, blew her nose, and stared at her toes.

"Would you believe? The Mid-gard Serpent never showed." She raised her head and glared at Jack. "The most important battle of all time, and the wretched worm goes hiding. Thor was beside himself, and Odin's curses blighted every tree in a hundred yards. They had a powwow with Hrym, who suggested we put off Ragnarok a week."

Jack turned off the oven, and put a cover over the frying pan. He didn't think Ronnie would want dinner any time soon.

"It sounds reasonable," he said. "There's no point in having an end-of-world battle if everyone isn't present."

"Reasonable? Reasonable! What's reasonable about it?" She didn't give him a chance to answer. "Today it's the Midgard Serpent. Last week it was the Fenris Wolf who didn't appear. The week before . . . it was," Ronnie paused and thought hard.

Jack prompted her.

"Sleipnir?"

She flung one heavy gauntlet across the room. It shattered a vase.

"Ja, Sleipnir. Odin couldn't find him, and no other steed would do. Every damn week someone goes missing. What's with everyone? Where's their responsibility?"

Ronnie threw her helmet upward, and it whizzed into the ceiling. A small shower of paint and plaster floated down, but the helmet remained stuck.

"I wouldn't miss Ragnarok for anything!"

Jack began to worry. If she slipped into a berserk rage, their house would suffer. As it were, he'd need a ladder to retrieve her helmet. He had to distract her before she ran amuck.

Clearing his throat, Jack said, "I installed a new handle on the Armory door."

Her chin drooped to her chest.

"Ja?"

She wasn't paying attention to him. Jack was losing her.

Jack motioned with his hands.

"It's this long."

She raised her head and stared at his hands.

"Ja?"

It was time to hit her with the special features.

"I installed a buzzer system for it. Press the button, and it automatically turns the handle to lock and unlock the door."

He demonstrated the motion by twirling his right hand back and forth.

Ronnie leaned forward, her body tensing.

"Ja?"

Time for the big one.

"Remember the bear grease Tyr gave us on our second anniversary? I used some on the door knob, so it has a smooth action."

She slipped out of her plate armor.

"I think I'll hang up my Apoc-alyptic Blue until next week." She glared at him for a moment. "Nothing stops Ragnarok then." Ronnie charged down the hallway.

Jack sat quietly until he heard her first moan. It was a good day. He saved the world, and he pleased his wife. He went into the master bedroom for his own reward. His computer was waiting for him.

Twins

by
Rosalia Sanfilippo

We hang from cliff's edge
Quiet
A dormant virus that percolates in peril
And feeds like a parasite.

The serpent swallows his own tail in a circling O
As he signals the end of times.
Will the universe stop expanding to snap
Like a rubber band back to primal nothing
Then stretch again a pregnant belly?
The scars are noticeable now.

Blue Krishna flashes before the white mountain
And guards the snowy top from a lotus flower.
Who reigns there?

The beaver will finish gnawing the Great Pole.
Save us! We wail to the heavens, to anyone who answers prayers.
Silence
The sun's fire burns our throat and we devour explosion.
We fear eternal nothing alone with dread
Holding hands ever tighter.

Unwanted Romulus and Remus abandoned in the sun.
Lupus nourishes, provides life.
But one twin kills the other. Cain kills Abel.
Death. Life.
Apollo and Artemis.
Kuat and Iae.
Ahriman and Ahura Mazda.
Sun and Moon, Good and Evil.

Jesus said, "Have you found the beginning, then,

That you are looking for the end? You see
The end will be where the beginning is."

He said, "Congratulations to the one who stands at the beginning. That one will know the end
and will not taste death."

Can we trust him?

A religious zealot smacks the grimace from your face
And thinks the doubt goes with it.
He fails to save even the worthiest
For he also is unworthy.

I don't let my spirit go.
I hold it captive
Inside my body.
Blink and the lights may go out.
But who can we listen to if not our own hearts?
Mine has been mute many years.
"Speak," I say and all I hear is a hum,
No words.

The end comes as a blinding flash in my dream.
I wake up wet-faced.
I only fear the time I don't wake
So shackle my life even tighter.
The end may have a twin, though.
The end –
The beginning.
Will we know the difference when it comes?

*

The Burden Of Sin

**by
Steve Redwood**

There can be only one. The Immortals must fight and decapitate each other until only one remains, and that one will inherit the power and wisdom of all the others.

What egregious nonsense! That idea, almost as ludicrous as the one that Immortals must not fight on holy ground, was cleverly put around by people fearful of our power if we combined, but unfortunately most of the Immortals believed it was true. And there was no escape even for those who didn't, since they were constantly forced to defend themselves against those who did, especially the headthirsty Scottish Highlands branch. I, however, managed to stay hidden for centuries, because I was the weakest—and therefore the least detectable—of all of us; even my runeblade, Wormclinger, though supposedly forged by an insane hunchback dwarf in Toledo, kept quiet, and would tremble if so much as a dirk or a poniard passed near. But in the end, when there were only two left, and the strong emanations of the other Immortals no longer hid my own scent, Hamish McLoud, who took it all far too seriously, began pursuing me all over the world, seeking to force me into combat.

"I killt yer brother Dmitri!" he yelled once, as I hid at the bottom of a disused mine-shaft, furious at the state my clothes were getting into. "You ha'e tae try tae avenge him! So then I can ha'e ye too!" Yes, it was true that McLoud killed Dimka in Madison Square Gardens in New York in 1986, but I didn't mind. He had been coarse and moronic, had never used a silk handkerchief in his life, and had spoken with the harsh accents of the Steppes. I had always been ashamed of having such an uncouth brute as a blood relative, and it was with a certain relief that I heard McLoud had lopped off his pustulous head; I even treated myself to a perfumed pedicure.

But it turned out Dimka had been the only other Immortal left, so McLoud, who had been occupied the previous five centuries fighting all the others, now turned his full decollatory obsession on me. Keeping on the move to escape him and his equally psychotic sword, Brawnblade, I slept in more beds than Yassir Arafat himself, even in some without clean sheets. For twenty-five years, McLoud tried to shame me into coming out of hiding. An enormous flag appeared on top of the

Taipei 101 building in Taiwan (the taller Burj Dubai Tower was destroyed in 2010, of course, with the rest of the Middle East), telling the world that "Foplamov is yellow-livered and spineless"; once he got access to the Queen's Christmas Message just before airing, and in her usual dead-parrot-like fashion she unblinkingly told her adoring and chomping subjects that "the British people must be brave i' the face of terror, which is mare than Foplamov is even when faced wi' a wee sleekit cow'rin' tim'rous beastie o' a mouse" ("Too much bloody time in Balmoral!" muttered the chomping subjects in Berkshire); when the Russian flag was unfurled on Mars, to the surprise of the cosmonauts, it warned the world, and any Russian-speaking Martians, that I was a smelly merkin on the retching pubis of the universe. It doesn't matter how stupid you are; if you have bank accounts accumulating interest for five hundred years, you have enough money to pay the right people to do almost anything.

Cowardice? It was a question of good taste and rationality, not cowardice. Fighting was the sort of thing only lowlife creatures did. Why should I risk my delicate skin battling a brute who not only picked his nose and ate the snot in public, but did it in front of a mosque before sundown in Ramadhan! A mad misogynist who founded and funded the John Knox Marriage Counselling Bureaus all over Scotland! A vulgar cretin who wore Marks & Sparks Y-fronts under his kilt—*and* back-to-front! Moreover, I knew I could never beat him in fair combat. While he and the others had spent hundreds of years doing nothing but strain and train and brain each other, I had treated the gift of immortality with more gratitude and respect. I had set out to enjoy life, not risk it. Wine, women, and wassailing; painting, poetry, and philosophy; mathematics, metafiction, and mythology. But especially I appreciated the aesthetic mentality. I reread Huysmans' *Against Nature* every month, whilst reclining on silk sheets, with Nubian princesses fallen on hard times relaxing my limbs, dear Oscar's portrait looking down upon me, caressing and languid music filling my ears. I was the most cultured man in the world, while McLoud remained a mere lout.

So for many years I ignored or avoided his puerile challenges, but with time it became impossible for me to do so. I ran out of safe houses. I began to suffer from travel-sickness. But, more important, I grew irritated. I found it aesthetically unpleasing to suffer such insults.

Late in 2012, I fished out my rusty, rotten, unused sword, Wormclinger.

My first impetuous idea was to silence McLoud forever in his sleep. After all, the fool never tried to hide his whereabouts. I knew he spent most of his time in St Andrews in Scotland, where he had long been addicted to golf.

But I soon realised it wouldn't be that easy. He would certainly have his defences against surprise attacks. Being immortal doesn't stop you getting killed, it simply means you resurrect each time. But getting killed in the first place is just as painful for an Immortal as it is for anyone else. Despite his brutish skill, even McLoud had been killed a couple of times, but, unfortunately for me, by mortals unaware they then needed to remove his head within thirty seconds before he returned to life; so *their* heads got removed instead. His whole place would be rigged with alarms, especially those set off by the proximity of sentient swords belonging to Immortals sneaking in through bedroom windows. I think he was aware that I was too cultured and superior to be slavishly bound by silly old-fashioned laws of chivalry.

No, I would have to lure him into a place of my own choosing, and also ensure he would be unable to defend himself; the last thing I wanted was a fair fight! I set myself to study his movements, his ideas, his history.

And found his weakness: John Knox was his childhood hero.

∏

January 2013. Allahabad, northern India. Fog and cold. The Maha Kumbh Mela, Great Pitcher Festival, came round once again, as it did every twelve years. Here, on the *Sangam*, the confluence of three sacred rivers—the Ganges, the Yamuna, and the mythic Karaswati (yes, one would expect two real rivers plus one mythical one to equal two real rivers, but you try telling a Hindu that!)—a good eighty million people congregated for a few weeks to wash away their sins in *Ganga ma*, Mother Ganga. They believed this was one of the places where Vishnu's trusty steed Garuda paused when being pursued by demons, and some of the nectar of the gods fell from the Pitcher to the ground. A good dip here, then, might not only bring them whatever they most wanted—money, children, a new sari, a date with a Bollywood superstar, social success—but, more important, free them from having to put up with any more lives. Prevent that dratted reincarnation. Save them from the cycle of death and rebirth. *He who drinks Ganga water that has been heated by the Sun's rays derives merit much greater than that which attaches to the vow of subsisting upon the wheat or grains of other corn picked up from cow dung.* That's the *Mahabharata* itself, really putting cow-dung-eating in its place!

As for me, I didn't care whether they got reincarnated or not, or what kind of life they might expect next time round. The important point was that here was the greatest collection of sin anywhere in the world! What interested me was where those sins went when they were washed away.

There could be only one logical answer: downriver.

I spent a couple of days there with the colourful pilgrims, joining them as they crossed on the pontoon bridges to the holy site, admiring the contrast between the dark blue waters of the deeper Yamuna and the grey sandy currents of the Ganges, pining for a decent T-bone steak, shivering a bit, but greatly enjoying the antics of the Naga sadhus. It tickled me that these completely insane characters, naked and covered in ashes, with filthy braided hair down to their bunions, chanting, mumbling, prancing, rocking, blowing conch shells, were regarded as holy men, and I greatly admired the Hindus' highly eccentric sense of humour. Mecca and the Vatican would be much more fun places with a few Sadhus to liven things up. I saw one who proved his holiness by publicly wrapping his penis round a stick every day, and another who'd held his right hand up in the air for 20 years. Not hard to guess which hand he used for pleasuring himself! Unless he was as over-endowed in his groin as he was under-endowed in his head. Given the sheer size of the celestial pantheon, I suppose it was just about possible one or two of the more feeble-minded gods might feel this was an intelligent and respectful way to approach the numinous, and behave benignly in return.

But finally I could put off the unpleasant task no longer. With fifty servants, all confirmed atheists, of course, to carry the equipment, I went a few miles downriver in the direction of Varanasi to a part where we would not be seen by too many people, and where those who did see us could be paid off to keep quiet. In any case, they would never suspect what we were up to.

We cast our nets.

Ganga ma, indeed! A slattern, if ever there was one! When we finally hauled the massive nets in after three days (at the point I'd chosen, the river was still over a mile wide), I almost despaired. With three or four million people going in the river every day (up to ten million on one of the "auspicious" days), that was a lot of washed-off sins, even if each person only sinned once, which was unlikely, as so many of the pilgrims were old. I conservatively multiplied by fifty. But a sin itself is tiny, even to the believer, invisible to the naked eye, although its effects may be enormous. I had, however, underestimated the sheer quantity of extraneous matter. We had to filter out the ashes of dead people (and frequently more than their ashes), burnt charcoal from the cremations, soggy marigolds, chromium drifting down from the leather industries in Kanpur, coins, lost beads, sperm from Shilpa Shetty fanatics, pictures of gods, turbans, regurgitated curries; but the worst was the turds, bobbing turds, bloated turds, blighted and blighting turds. Nearly nine percent of the world's population live in the Indo-Gangetic Plain. That's a lot of turds. Not *all* of them end up in the rivers . . . After five days' stomach-churning labour, we had panned down to a few dozen containers of a thick fluid a bit like runny mucus supposedly painted red by a stubborn daltonic dwarf.

But even this was still not pure sin. It was contaminated with flecks of remorse, twinges of conscience, fleeting desires of reparation and expiation, wisps of prayer, and other impurities.

Removing that gunge got us down to less than half a pint. But it was half a pint of the most concentrated, heinous, foul and vile sin that had ever existed, the mere thought of which would have given the Devil himself an instant orgasm, if he had existed.

I was ready to face Hamish McLoud.

∏

I had initially assumed that he lived in St Andrews in order to play golf every day. (He certainly wasn't there to be near the University!) But that wasn't the only, or perhaps even the main, reason. Hamish McLoud, thug, brute, obsessed decapitator, was a Believer! And a Believer in the worst form of the Christian God! Very early in his life he came heavily under the influence of the Scottish reformer John Knox, with the paradoxical result that although he was Immortal, he believed in Hell, but wasn't sure whether he was one of the Elect or one of the Damned. Good works, according to Knox, would have no effect: either you were buggered or not buggered. Knox selfishly died before the terrified boy could find out from him which he was. But McLoud never forgot him. My investigations revealed to me that even now every Sunday without fail he would go to Holy Trinity Church in South Street: this had been the town's old kirk, and the reason it attracted him, it seemed, was because it was precisely from here that Knox, in between fulminating against the monstrous regiment of women, in 1559 had incited the congregation to ransack and raze the Cathedral.

It was from these few facts I hatched my plan.

Although I naturally didn't believe in the *theological* concept of sin, McLoud obviously did. Things that would make me smile would lie heavily on his conscience. My own 'sins' and those of others weighed as lightly for me as promises to repay borrowed money, as dutiful kisses blown in a hurricane, but those same sins for McLoud were real and measurable and palpable: a burden that if big enough might even send him to Hell. So my plan had been to scoop up and collect the greatest possible amount of sin, and where better than at Allahabad, where tens of millions of people would obligingly leave their sins to float away in the Ganges? And not just the sins of one lifetime, but possibly those of previous incarnations as well. That is why I had to work only with unbelievers; belief *in the effects* of those sins would make their sheer mass and weight unmanageable. By the time I finished, I had a distillation so potent, so dense, that even for me who didn't believe in its existence it had physical weight! To McLoud that weight would be a million times greater.

I sent word to him; challenged him to mortal combat at midnight in the grounds of the old castle ruins at St. Andrews; a fitting site, I said, as his gushing blood would be added to that of so many other Scots who were slain there; and by losing his repulsive head so near to home, his compatriots could admire it the following day spiked to the remaining castle wall! That, I knew, was the kind of taunting language he would understand, and would be unable to ignore.

He gleefully accepted the challenge, of course.

Although my plan was perfect, I still found I was nervous as I approached the castle, just before the appointed time. At the last moment I hesitated. If my information about McLoud's beliefs were wrong, or my calculations, or if something prevented me from carrying out the plan . . . No, it was now or never! No longer would I put up with his jibes and public assassinations of my character! I repressed my fears, and using a rope ladder I brought with me, hauled myself over the castle walls.

It was a blustery March night. A cold sea mist hung over the grounds, shrouding off the rest of the town, but still allowing occasional obscure glimpses of a low moon constantly shredded by scudding clouds. Below the promontory, the Atlantic thrashed in anticipation against the rocks as if it were a vast noisy audience of sea monsters trying to scramble up the cliff to see the blood spectacle. Their salty breath poured in over the seaward walls carrying the memories of ghost ships and drowned mariners and depths where no light ever penetrated.

He was already there waiting. In full regalia, with the stridently exaggerated tartan of his clan. Brawnblade still sheathed, but the burnished dragon hilt alone emanating so much menace I felt Wormclinger trembling against my thigh. Full beard, broad chest, proud stance. Right hand already gauntleted.

I checked my jacket pocket for the hundredth time.

"Ach, Vasily Foplamov, so we meet at last! I didnae think ye'd hae the courage. But there can be only yin. I am glad ye hae decided after all tae die like a true warrior! As yer brother did."

I forced what I hoped was a grim smile, and called up one of the clichés I had prepared to make him think I would follow the idiotic rules of these duels.

"My brother was too headstrong, and apt to lose his head in a crisis, but be assured I do not intend to lose mine. I have come to avenge him, and cleanse the family honour!"

McLoud obviously liked that, and almost beamed with satisfaction: this was the tone all midnight mortal combats ought to have. I wondered how many times he had watched *Rob Roy* or *Braveheart*.

"Bold words," he declaimed, his booming voice making the mist cringe, "but are ye ready tae back them up wi' bold deeds?"

"That, you will soon see, Hamish McLoud," I riposted, with an epideictic curling of my lip and tilting of my chin, "but that will be the last you *will* see! My unforgiving blade Wormclinger, imbued with all the terrible magic of the celebrated insane dwarfs of Toledo, will then cloud your vision for ever!" (I thought I heard a small still voice near my thigh muttering, *Do we have to go through with this?*)

McLoud chuckled with delight. God, the man was a moron!

"Many a man hae sought tae cross blades wi' Hamish McLoud, and none hae lived tae tell the tale, because Brawnblade, once wielded by the Tricky Cross-eyed Samurai Oda Hideyoshi his self, drinks souls like sassenachs drink weak tea!" He waited expectantly.

I couldn't take any more of this. My cultivated sensibilities were squirming with embarrassment.

"Then," said I, "my strong right arm must avenge them too, as well as my brother. But," casually putting my left hand in my pocket, and drawing out a pewter flask, "fighting is thirsty work. First, allow me to wet my lips in anticipation of a glorious and thrilling combat." I began to unstopper the flask.

"Och aye, ye'd be seeking a wee dram o' courage, and I dinnae blame thee for tha'!"

I moved nearer to him, extending the now open flask towards him, as if in offering.

"Perchance you wish to imbibe your last drink ever?"

"Nay, a McLoud has no need o' . . ."

His voice was cut off as I suddenly hurled the contents of the flask at him. I had meant to throw them full in his face, but the rather narrow neck of the flask caused the liquid to fall short, most of it only landing on his chest, and even a few large splashes on me.

But the effect was immediate. It was as if he had been hit by a pile driver; he gasped and collapsed to the ground. He tried to rise, but it seemed a tremendous weight was holding him down. I moved to stand over him. *Bless you, John Knox!* McLoud stared up at me, agony and disbelief in his eyes.

"What . . . what hae ye done tae me?"

I poured the liquid that still remained in the flask over his legs. I heard the bones breaking with the weight.

"Sin, McLoud, sin. The sins of millions of people, all distilled and concentrated just for you. A weight no true believer could ever bear." I shook the remaining drops out of the flask. "And now I bid you goodbye. Let me give you a head start on your journey to Hell!"

I unsheathed and raised Wormclinger, ready to remove the head of the man who had tormented me for so long. The ancient runeblade began to descend . . .

. . . and stopped, screeching as if in mortal agony, bare inches from McLoud's neck. I felt a recoil force in my arms as if I had struck rock. I dropped the sword in pain. McLoud stirred, trying to rise, trying to reach for his own sword. I picked up Wormclinger again—I had the impression it was trying to wriggle away—once more prepared to strike —and once more some unseen force interposed between the blade and the neck.

McLoud, his face twisted by the weight of the sin pressing on him, forced a rictus that might have been an attempt at a smile.

"Ye fool," he gasped, "this is holy ground. Immortals cannae fight nae kill on holy ground."

His laugh was like a boulder being splashed by an underground waterfall.

"This isn't holy ground! This is a castle! The Cathedral's over there!"

McLoud laughed again, even as I heard more bones cracking.

"Bishops, archbishops lived here. Fer centuries. And martyr's blood . . . Reformation . . . Wishart burnt at stake here. Others. Forest. Hamilton. The ground remembers, och aye, the ground remembers. Relics of St. Andrew his self nearby . . . Not holy?"

What was happening? If the ground itself wasn't allowing Wormclinger to do its work, it meant that holy ground was indeed different from normal ground, had unnatural power. In which case . . .

Even before I had thought the unthinkable, I felt sharp pains all over my body, as if tiny but potent hammer blows were raining down upon me. I gasped with the pain.

I tried to force away the sudden realisation. If I were stupid enough to even *begin* to believe in holy ground, then I would also have to believe in the same sin crushing McLoud *because of* his belief.

The rain of blows increased. Heavier, deeper. I was forced to my knees. It was the sin that had splashed on me when I had thrown the contents of the flask over my enemy. I had barely noticed it at the time, because I didn't believe in sin . . . but as belief seeped into me like a deadly toxin, so the true weight of the sin on me increased.

At the same time I felt myself being dragged closer to the man writhing on the ground. Dragged by an invisible force. Oh God in Heaven! Not only was the weight of the sin beginning to crush me as it had crushed McLoud, but that same weight was increasing the gravitational force between us. And the more force it exerted, the more I had no choice but to believe in the unbearable weight of the distilled sin of millions of people from another continent, and the more I believed . . .

I felt the ground rise up around us as the laws of Newton and God combined, and my enemy and I, the last two Immortals, began our long inseparable journey to the centre of the earth.

Cracking Nuts With Jan Hammer

by
Rhys Hughes

Progressive rock musicians. Where do they go after they die? They go to Hell, that's where, to a corner reserved just for them. I know this for sure because I was a prog rock musician, then I died and began the long slide down to Hell, where I am now.

What happened was that the instant after my death, a flight of steps appeared in the ground, a spiral staircase without a visible base, but it had a bannister running alongside it, and I had a sudden urge to straddle that bannister and corkscrew to the bottom, and that's what I did and thus I reached Hell, where I still am.

Not everybody who ends up in Hell gets there like that. Prog rockers nearly always do, nobody knows why.

People wonder what it's like down here. It's Hell.

That doesn't mean it's unbearable. It's unpleasant rather than nasty. There's a lot of resentment among my fellow sufferers because nobody ever told them that prog rock was a sin.

Some of them still don't think it is. Others even deny they were prog rockers in the first place.

Take Jan Hammer for instance. He won't stop making speeches about how the music he played in the Mahavishnu Orchestra and other bands was fusion jazz rather than prog. He writes long letters to the Devil explaining the difference between the two styles.

The Devil never answers. Damned if I know why.

The crux of Jan Hammer's argument is that fusion jazz was played by jazz musicians who were attracted to rock music while prog rock was played by rock musicians attracted to jazz.

I doubt he'll get anywhere with that approach.

I guess the term 'prog rock' is defined by excessive length of songs, unnecessary time changes, difficult keys, unusual rhythms, obscure lyrics, self indulgent solos and heavy use of electricity rather than the precise cultural history of the players.

That's probably how the Devil sees it. And he should know. He has all the best tunes, or so it's said.

On the other hand, or claw, it could be that he's simply ignorant but doesn't care. If he's truly the Lord of Chaos it's unlikely he spends time agonising over the precise meaning of terms. His album collection probably isn't even in alphabetical order.

It hardly matters one way or the other.

I know Jan Hammer's complaints off by heart. Down here in this corner of Hell we have to work in pairs, preparing snacks for musicians who play any type of music *other* than prog rock. Jan Hammer is my partner. Our main job is to crack nuts. Sometimes we prepare canapés or dishes of olives and other pickles, rarely cheese and biscuits. But nuts are our speciality. We crack all kinds but pistachios are the most common by far. Since my demise I must have cracked a billion nuts.

Jan Hammer has cracked even more. Time is not the same down here as above. One of our years can fit inside one of your seconds. Decades of cracking nuts, centuries, millennia. That's our punishment, our punishment for our concept albums and gatefold sleeves. Disproportionate, I hear you cry? Yes I agree it's very unfair.

What was that? The sentence should be even harsher?

I think you're a swine and probably in the pay of the Devil. How can you be so cruel to someone you don't even know? And that reminds me, no introductions have yet been made.

I already know who you are. You are the reader.

Now I'll tell you who I am. My name is Anthony Lewis. I was the lead singer of a prog rock band called Satori. We never made it big in the prog world like Yes, Genesis or Jethro Tull. We came on the scene too late; two and a half decades too late if truth be told. Or if you prefer truth not to be told, we were ahead of our time.

We underwent some personnel changes, as all bands do, not just prog rock bands, but our quintessential lineup was Stuart, Lee, Steve, John and myself out front. I am not tall, not slim, but my voice is astounding. My mortal enemy, Huw Rees, told me I don't have the charisma to get away with what I attempt on stage. This criticism baffled me. I never attempted anything too theatrical or melodramatic. My efforts to engage the audience were ironic, playful, sparse. I just wanted to sing and that's what I did, without frills and only one hat.

Huw Rees played drums for folk bands.

Satori played prog rock at a time when almost nobody else was capable of structuring a song that lasted longer than three minutes. I still think that's something to be proud of.

The Devil has appalling taste. That's why he's the Devil.

He relishes the sort of music that was ubiquitous when I was alive on the circuit: lazy folk rock, singer songwriters crooning sentimental words to simple strummed chords on an acoustic guitar, young girls and boys with names like Maria, Tracy, Damien or Jeff. The city where my band was based, Swansea, was awash with acts like that. The Devil must rate Swansea as one of his favourite music hangouts.

In some ways I'd rather be here in Hell.

It's much worse for Jan Hammer, of course. He was a big star in his day, highly respected, quite wealthy. He could afford to live in any city he liked: Miami, Prague, London, Paris. He knew the good life. Hell is a considerable drop in standards for him. That's why he still hopes he can escape his destiny, argue his way back to the surface, insist he has been bracketed in the wrong musical category. But only one reprieve from Hell has ever been issued since the origin of reality and the chances of him earning another are negligible.

No, he's stuck with me, Anthony Lewis, forever.

The other reason he'll never be set free is that he's a superlative cracker of nuts. A really fine nutcracker. He can crack ten nuts with his ten fingers all at once, as if he's playing a really big pistachio chord, or he can crack them in rapid succession, like a really fast arpeggio, or he can crack them under the toes of his shoes, the same way he pushed down on an effects pedal to modulate the output of his synthesiser on some of those early Mahavishnu recordings. No nut has been cracked properly if it hasn't been cracked by Jan Hammer.

The musicians who eat them don't understand.

I detest having to crack nuts for bands who sound like Joy Division, The Cure or Oasis. I don't think they deserve them. Nor do they deserve the stuffed vine leaves, pitta bread or houmous that other prog rock pairs are condemned to prepare for them.

Jan Hammer claims to have access to the internet. There's a hole in the ceiling of the little room where we sleep and occasionally I agree to help him climb inside it. I crouch and he stands on my shoulders and grips the edges of the hole with his skilled fingers and takes his own weight as much as he can bear and then I slowly rise, pushing the soles of his feet and the rest of him upwards and after lots of puffing he manages to enter the hole and vanishes for an hour.

There's a computer in that cavity and Jan Hammer uses it to look up facts and rumours about the Devil. A lot of potentially useful data can't pass the firewalls of Hell but enough gets through to give us an inkling of why the Devil hates prog rock. It has nothing to do with any inherent flaw in the music itself or any law of the cosmos. It's purely personal. It seems the Devil had an upsetting experience while listening to Gentle Giant's fourth album. The upsetting experience itself remains a mystery. I suspect it was something to do with finding out a friend had betrayed him, that's the standard reason.

I have never entered that cavity. I don't fit.

I don't really believe a computer exists up there. Whether through stress or mischief, Jan Hammer often tells lies to me, lies that are so ludicrous they might form part of some obscure test. Once he told me the drummer Carl Palmer was a saint and his cymbals were spare halos. But I've glimpsed Carl Palmer down here in Hell and I know he was merely a prog rocker like the rest of us.

In fact I've seen all of ELP. It happened a few weeks ago when I went to empty the bins that were full of nut shells. I glanced into a room as I walked down a passage and I saw Keith Emerson forcing slices of pineapple and cubes of cheese onto little sticks. He was working with Greg Lake. It is rare that musicians who played together on the surface are permitted to stay together in Hell. Maybe this was an extra punishment for the pair of them. In that case, the Devil has got it right for once. When I returned along the passage they had gone.

The Devil does regularly move us around. This is to keep us unsettled and agitated. The next time Jan Hammer and I are relocated we'll lose the internet connection that probably doesn't exist anyway. That's a shame. I would love to email all my friends and colleagues who are still living, especially the surviving members of Satori, to warn them. The only other option is to visit the surface, a privilege very difficult to earn. Just one working pair are awarded that honour for one hour every year and each time it goes to Darryl Way from Curved Air and Peter Hammill from Van der Graaf Generator. I don't know why.

Not long after I first arrived I went to see the Devil, to clarify my rights and obligations during my stay. I set out with high hopes but after a journey of many nights I was stopped by a sentry guarding a door of ice set into a wall of molten iron that somehow kept its shape. The Devil was in a meeting, I was informed, but a brief audience might be possible with his secretary, the squat helium voiced designer lesbian, Julie Burchill. I declined the offer. Behind the ice, a bulky shadow pressed its bare thighs to the chilly translucency. I retraced my steps and so began my afterlife in perdition with Jan Hammer.

I now wonder if the Devil is a prisoner.

Nobody ever sees him; nobody hears from him directly. His wishes are passed to us in scribbled messages, yellow memos we can stick only on our walls, for there are no fridge doors down here. It might be that Julie Burchill or someone like her runs the entire show, in the same way Martin Bormann controlled the final days of the Reich by reinterpreting Hitler's orders according to his own agenda. It's not infeasible that the Devil is completely ignorant of what is happening in his realm. He might even be a fan of Supertramp or Steely Dan.

If Milton was allowed to fantasise about him, so can I, Anthony Lewis of Satori. I don't intend to glorify him, nor even to forgive him, but he deserves at least as much of a fair hearing as Andy Latimer's guitar work on Camel's debut album, an underrated release with a fine cover. If by any slim chance he's a prog rock fan . . .

No, I'm getting carried away now, falling into the trap of pretending some sort of mistake has been made, that I shouldn't really be here. It's what I criticise Jan Hammer for. I'm more realistic than that. I'm in Hell for my crimes and that's that.

Back to cracking nuts, I guess. Tedious.

Jan Hammer is in a talkative mood today. He keeps firing questions at me. Do I think that the 'Canterbury Sound' pioneered by such bands as The Soft Machine, Matching Mole and Caravan is a subset of prog or a separate category? If a separate category, why hasn't fusion jazz been accorded the same distinction? Is art rock identical to prog rock and if not, why not? Are the members of Henry Cow in Hell preparing snacks? What about outfits like Can, Faust and Cluster? Do they escape the prog label simply because they influenced electronic dance music? I don't care about the answers to any of these pointless riddles.

The only musicians I've seen down here so far apart from Jan Hammer, ELP, Darryl Way and Peter Hammill are Chris Squire and Rick Wakeman from Yes, Neil Peart from Rush, Tony Reeves from Greenslade, Christian Vander from Magma, Euan Lowson from Pallas and Dave Stewart from Egg. Maybe we're the only ones in Hell to date. Perhaps King Crimson and Pink Floyd found a loophole. There are too many questions, too many unresolved issues. But I am Anthony Lewis.

That's the only certainty I'm left with.

My lyrics made a lot more sense than Jon Anderson's ever did. I wrote a song that was a history of the entire universe, not a concept album but a single song. That shows conciseness as well as grandiosity. I remember a few lines from it too. The sulphurous clouds of Hell haven't fully addled my senses yet. Not yet . . . *370 million years ago / the forests took over the land (you heard about it) / About the same time cats appeared . . .* That's how it went in part. It's not entirely accurate. Forests came long before cats and both came long before prog.

But it's music. I was an entertainer.

Jan Hammer insists instrumentals are superior to songs. I wonder if he thinks pistachios are better than cashews? It's all academic. I don't mean academic in a good way, with professors debating it and writing papers on the theme, but pointless. That's the only sort of academic there is in Hell. Learning stops here.

I worry about the other members of Satori. I dream about them touring the venues of Swansea, paying homage to me every time they mount the stage and dedicating each song to my memory, and I want to rise out of Hell and shake them and shout at them to stop playing prog rock, to warn them their souls are in danger if they continue. But in my dreams all my cries are swamped by Lee's elaborate saxophone lines, John's technical drumming, Steve's fancy keyboard work and Stuart's fiddly bass. I wake with a sweat slicking my furrowed brow, that forehead that knows no fringe, and the bad thing about waking with such a sweat from such a dream in Hell is that the sweats of the day are even worse.

Look me up on the internet. I'm Anthony Lewis. Of Satori fame. Fame without fortune. Fortune without fame. In fact I've never known either. I just kept singing under my hat.

The only reprieve won from Hell was for Brian Eno.

I think that's fair enough . . .

If he was a prog rocker then the Penguin Café Orchestra was staffed with real penguins. And the Devil gigs with the Pope. But Jan Hammer is still offended by Eno's release.

I mention it as infrequently as I can.

At this very moment he's outside in the passage cocking his ear at a distant rumble. But he's still cracking pocketfuls of nuts with his hands. Something is racing towards us.

It's getting bigger. I wonder if it's a giant bun. Jan Hammer once told me that he watched Chris Squire throw a giant bun around the solar system. Undoubtedly another lie.

Whatever it is, here it comes now.

To my complete astonishment a memo arrives on one of those handcarts that are the only vehicles allowed in Hell. These handcarts move around on their own but don't appear to be remote controlled. I'm sure they operate themselves and perhaps are sentient creatures. I have said that I arrived in Hell on a bannister like other prog rockers, but certain people descend on these handcarts, chiefly men and women who forget to pay their bills or who gamble away inheritances.

Satori's inheritance must never be gambled.

The memo is full of good news. Because of our dedication to cracking nuts, both qualitatively and quantitatively, the privilege of ascending to Earth for an hour has been awarded to us instead of Darryl Way and Peter Hammill. I'm delighted by this, but it doesn't really help me warn all the surviving members of Satori. Being sent to the surface is not a holiday as such. We still have to work.

The lucky pair who get an hour on the surface have to go in disguise and never reveal their identities to living people. They also have to take up crates of snacks with them.

Another handcart comes for us and we climb into it. The fit is very tight because of all the nuts and tortillas that take up most of the room. Suddenly a spiral bannister appears from nowhere and the handcart attaches itself over it and we begin accelerating upwards. Just like riding a monorail, not that I ever have.

We might end up anywhere, in any land or on any planet where music is a phenomenon. Maybe Calcutta, Helsinki, Los Angeles, Uranus, Ursa Major, Andromeda or even other universes: Blubberhack, Greasewrinkle. Who knows? At the exact moment we reach the ceiling and I think we are about to have our dead brains dashed out on solid rock, a hole opens and closes like a mouth and we are above again.

By an improbable coincidence we are in Swansea.

I conceal my ecstasy and set about unloading the nuts and tortillas. We are in a back room of a venue called *The Chattery* and I can't wait to get out front and see if anyone I know is there. I'm hoping against hope that Stuart, Lee, John or Steve will be present so I can whisper my words of warning and save their souls!

When the nuts and tortillas have been dealt with, we cautiously make our way into the main room. The small stage has been set up with a small keyboard and a microphone. Something simple is obviously the order of the night. We sit and wait near the back. Within five minutes, to my delight, the survivors of Satori really do come in. I let them settle down before I lean over to break the news.

Disaster strikes! Jan Hammer loses control!

Something has compelled him to leave his seat and position himself in front of the keyboard. I see what he is about to do but it's too late to stop him. So I prioritise the passing of my message to my old colleagues. I whip off my disguise and gleam baldly.

Prog rock will condemn you to Hell, I shriek!

They exchange amused glances. Then they tell me that within an hour of my death they stopped playing prog and started playing other kinds of music, individually and collectively. I was the only reason they played prog rock in the first place. They don't need my warning, their souls are already safe. I am devastated by this revelation. It fills me with mixed emotions in the same way that a bag of pistachios, cashews, almonds and pecans is full of fighting flavours.

The only satisfaction I get is the news that the only prog rocker in Swansea is Huw Rees. At some point he has changed allegiance. I find that incredibly ironic and I laugh.

But this means he will someday join me in Hell.

So I stop laughing quickly!

A sudden blast of noise diverts all our attentions to the stage. Jan Hammer is helping himself to the gig. The young singer-songwriter due to come on and croon her numbers has been usurped by a grizzled virtuoso! She stands uncertainly at the bar.

Jan Hammer has launched into a dazzling sequence of arpeggios, grace notes and wibbly wobbly tweakings.

He makes a face like he's being eaten.

That's what the Devil will surely do to him later, when he finds out. Or if not the Devil then Julie Burchill. I don't envy Jan Hammer. He is committing the ultimate anti-sin.

All offences against the Devil are anti-sins.

A terrible thought has struck me. I am still suffused with complex emotions, the simultaneous feeling that I've been betrayed by my friends and relief that they are safe.

Characters in stories don't have such complex emotions. A slim hope I've always entertained that I might not be the real Anthony Lewis but a caricature in a satirical tale by an author I know has now been denied. I must be the real Anthony Lewis!

I have nothing to look forward to in this case. Just an eternity of cracking nuts and maybe being paired up with someone even worse than Jan Hammer such as Geddy Lee or the yodeller from Focus, Thijs van Leer. Every time I sigh there is the smell of worms. Not because I'm dead but because I'm waiting with baited breath. To see what the Devil might do. He hasn't done anything yet. I check the time.

Twenty five minutes before we have to return to Hell. Jan Hammer has just finished an enormous solo. He looks like he's about to launch into another ambitious tune. A spark of rebellion jumps up inside me and bursts into flame. I jump up too and grab the microphone on stage. Now there's only twenty four minutes left.

Just enough time for a song about the history of the entire universe!

Murk

by Robert Lamb

Despite the pain, a pain that seemed to form the outer boundaries of an ever-growing numbness, Nathan Griggs continued his slow, shambling decent into the subway system. Relying heavily on the hand rail, bracing himself for balance with each labored step, he shuffled his increasingly unmanageable girth down the stairs.

One after the other, he told himself. *The left, then the right . . .*

The weight made it difficult. Movements which had come second nature to him all his life now took concentration, strained effort to accomplish. He'd only had a few days to adjust to it.

He took another step, slid his oily hands down the railing.

There was a thunder of footfalls behind him, giving him just a moment's warning before three teenagers stampeded past him, taking two steps at a time in their high-end sneakers as they rushed down to the terminal.

One of their shoulders caught him in the side and he swayed, desperately tightening his grip on the rail. His knees buckled, but he managed to keep his balance long enough to pull himself into the wall.

The kids cackled as they vanished around the corner of the next landing. Griggs was sure he heard "fat fuck" somewhere in the mix of slang and laughter, but they were already just an echo.

A final tremble of vertigo shivered through him before equilibrium returned. His cheek pressed flat against the wall, he exhaled his relief in a fog of moisture across the grimy yellow tiles.

He used to wonder if this place had ever really been clean. As a younger, healthier man, he'd gazed into the grime and envisioned the cement floors having been poured from the belly of some tainted mine, each tile set in mortar scooped from the lungs of cancer-ridden behemoths. Every surface felt chillingly alive with microscopic activity —occasionally sticky with an unknowable, infectious glaze.

It was amazing how one's perspective on what was acceptable could shift over night—change entirely in the course of two weeks.

Still holding the railing, he heaved himself out from the wall. He took another step down, then another, just as the first arrivals began hurrying their way up from the terminal—packs of rushing youths first, one older, Japanese man in a spiffy suit. None of them seemed to notice the morbidly obese figure on the stairs.

Fat fuck.

Then came the walkers—assorted races, assorted positions on the socioeconomic sorting shelf—they all moved steadily past him, up the stairway to the surface and sun. He made a point of not looking at them, tried not to engage them anymore than the mere sight of him was likely to.

Thankfully, many of them were already half-submerged in another place—the cords of hidden iPods slithering up to plug their ears with banal tunes and rhythm. How long till those little white plugs stoppered nostrils against the stench? How long til they filled the mouth like a ball gag and packed gouged-out sockets with sights of the better-than and wish-it-were?

He still felt their gaze, though, felt them eye-fucking him through their peripherals. A lone Chinese woman lugged grocery bags that reeked of dead sea life. A punk girl with a face full of piercings carried a baby in her arms. Their youthful vigor hit him like poison. When the girl finally glanced at him, her eyes burned the question into him: *How could you let that happen to you?*

By the time he'd made it down to the next landing, the last of the new arrivals were surfacing: a few elderly loners, a bum. Last of all, a sallow-faced transit cop walked past him with the kind of deliberate inattention only an off-duty police could muster.

The noise of their footfalls followed them up the stairs, fading until he was alone again.

Griggs stared up into the circular, convex mirror in the corner of the landing, positioned near the ceiling, at his own murky reflection. His shabby, gaunt face was ridiculously disproportionate to the bloated torso that belled out around him under the trench coat. His eyes were bloodshot and bagged, his sunken cheeks covered with a week's worth of scraggly stubble.

The echoes of the trains rose up to him.

He felt weary—felt at one with the sickness that covered every surface of the underground. But there wasn't that much further to go. One more flight, through the turn sties and then he could take a piss before the final decent.

Then you can sit, he told himself. *Then you can finally rest.*

He had to know. He had to bring the circle back around to what happened two weeks and 180 pounds ago. He knew the answers were down there in the tunnels, down where the trains wormed their way through the guts of the city.

Currently, it was all a blur—a jumbled dustbin of fragmented memories.

It had been sometime after 5 a.m., on his ride home from another graveyard shift of IT work, the tail end of another empty night flipping monitors.

He'd been one of only five passengers in that particular subway car. He'd taken his usual empty-hours seat in the middle of the isle, pulled out one of those hipster magazines he occasionally picked up at work. There was an article in it about the war, another about global warming and—more his speed at 5 a.m.—an artsy photo shoot with some lush, 20-something in latex. She'd been photographed squatting over a silver bowl with a beef tongue in one hand and a machete in the other. The blade had been inscribed with three symbols, something like "NNX."

One moment he'd just been sitting there, lost in the woman's curves. The next, a jolt rattled everything to the core.

A groan of metal.

A tremor shaking through the spine of the train.

Something like greenish-black ink splattering across the outside of the windows.

The rest was hazy.

He remembered screams, the sound of something thudding against the roof of the car. There was a great deal of breaking glass and twisting metal—then only darkness.

Later, the doctors had told him he'd been trapped in the wreckage for six hours—just lying there unconscious in the dark while emergency responders made their way down. The surface world had tittered with rumors of terrorism. The nurses had told him it was a miracle he'd survived unscathed. After one more night of surveillance, they released him back to the wife and kids.

Five days later, he'd sent them all to stay with Gail's mother upstate.

∏

He was lucky enough to find the restroom both unlocked and unattended—a rarity these days. He stuffed himself into the last stall and, once again, resisted the urge to sit down and relieve his aching frame of its ponderous burden. Instead, he leaned against the concrete wall and set his fingers to work unfastening the front of his trench coat.

His actual waist had been somewhat absorbed by the swelling, but he'd managed to secure his pants by simply lashing them tightly just above his groin. He reached blindly under the enormous bulge of his belly, finally rolling his chill-shrunken member out through the zipper.

For a while, he just stood there—thinking about urination, opening the mental valves and pawing with his mind at the triggers of release.

He reached underneath the XXXL t-shirt with his other hand and, in what had become a familiar gesture in these final days, felt the surface of his belly. The skin was hard with swelling, just a membrane of pressure and pain coating an enormity of numbness. The more he ran his hand across his gut, the more he could feel the individual balls of globular tissue inside him.

He had convinced himself it was just some manner of water retention at first, maybe stress-related weight gain, but eventually there could be little doubt it was a tumor.

He'd Googled up a host of worrisome images: gaunt men and women with enormous sacks of flesh ballooning out of their side, human eyes staring piteously out of faces twisted into bloated mockeries. It spiraled into blood-slick surgical photos, the elephant man's tortured skeleton. He learned the arteries inside larger growths could swell to the thickness of water hoses, the host shriveled and starving as the rouge tissue gorged itself on blood.

He'd panicked—and somehow, through the panic, had been able to convince himself nothing was wrong, as only a man facing the sudden onset of malignancy can do.

The swelling had continued. It wasn't long before Gail was pleading with him to see a doctor.

On the fifth day, the globular nature of the tissue had become apparent. His energy had waned and he was finally forced to give into the shame and quit going to work altogether.

At last he'd sent the family away for the weekend. He'd told Gail he needed a couple of days to himself and that Monday, he'd go to the doctor. He'd told himself he'd think it through, just needed the time to process it all alone.

He'd left the apartment Sunday night and purchased several bottles of vodka before checking into a cheap hotel room—a place to imprison his apprehensions, calm the terror growing inside him.

The spells of lightheadedness had begun to hit him whenever he made sudden movements, sending his mind reeling in backward summersaults, splitting a hundred different directions. And it wasn't just the spins or vertigo either—that he'd recognize. This was nothing short of a sudden leap through the kaleidoscope. It made him feel as if his mind were pouring out through a thousand different holes, into a thousand different possibilities, then back into himself, back into his squalid bed in room 308.

His skin had crept in revulsion at the thought of arteries the size of sausages, and he'd tried to drown the mental image in vodka.

He'd pondered over the bottle of sleeping pills on the night stand and watched black-and-white footage of the invasion of Normandy through a blood-shot haze, numbed himself with Cartoon Network and Animal Planet till reality began to seep into a Technicolor blur.

But it had only gotten worse.

Tuesday, the drink had just curtled to anger and self-loathing in his gut. In a rage, he'd grabbed one of the globs of tissue and squeezed it until he could feel it burst under the skin. He wasn't sure what he'd expected—perhaps the release of popping a zit or pulling out a splinter. He'd certainly felt the pressure shift inside, but it immediately turned into the sharpest pain he could remember, shattering through the numbness. His mind had performed another back flip, fragmenting a hundred ways through a sea of pain. He'd shrieked. He'd trembled. He'd wept. He'd had more to drink and turned up the volume on the idiot box.

He'd grown more depressed after that. The tumors had continued to grow. His reflection was staggering to behold. He'd finally tried a couple of the sleeping pills with the booze. The darkness had taken him for a spell.

He must have slept all of Thursday and maybe part of Friday. He'd woken to the sound of animated characters chasing each other around a ship, wondering if Gail was looking for him, imagined her showing up at the door with some cop and the hotel clerk. The thought of her finding him like this had terrified him. He'd spent a large portion of that afternoon shuffling a pile of pills around his cupped hands, weeping uncontrollably.

That night he'd dreamt through the kaleidoscope again—dreamt of running through a hundred underground tunnels, up through the base of the worldspine and towards the sun.

Rise, he'd heard a thousand voices whispering in his mind, *rise . . .*

At last he felt the slight release of urine trickling out of him, heard the sweet music of it splashing against yellowed porcelain.

∏

Griggs shuffled out of the restroom stall, only glancing at the crimson cloud he'd left dispersing in the bowl. Slowly, applying great care to each footfall, he made his way down the last couple of flights to the terminal itself.

He braced himself against one of the oily support beams—this one with a skull-studded sticker for a band called MAETH plastered to it—and began waiting for the train.

He'd made this decision just 24 hours ago, day 14 of his new life. Back in room 308, he'd eaten the last of the pizza. The liquor was running low. The pills were tempting him more and more to just fold the fucking cards, close up shop and let someone else worry with his mess.

"But why here?" he had asked himself. "Why now when don't know how? Don't know why?"

His pill and booze-numbed mind had fumbled with wild theories: radioactive waste stored under the city, a terrorist's dirty bomb, something in the air down there perhaps, gasses rising up through the cracks . . . The question had burned its way through his mind and he'd felt his desire for understanding move through a hundred different tunnels of consciousness. He had imagined the subway car twisting through the massive, tumor-swollen veins of the earth. He had thought back to the greenish-sludge flowing over the windows, of the screaming, crashing glass and rattling steel that filled the murky void between wreck and recovery.

So he'd decided to take the final journey of his unspectacular little life—to leave his lair of self-destruction in room 308 and return to wherever it was on that dotted, crimson line beneath the city that everything had changed.

He felt the tremor of the train approaching, heard its roar advancing before it through the darkness of the tunnel.

He looked down and saw a rat crawling its way across the garbage-strewn tracks, moving haphazardly toward his side of the terminal. It paused here and there to inspect the surrounding refuse: coffee cups, cigarette butts, newspaper scraps already beginning to dance in the ozone wind of the approaching train.

And everywhere there were batteries. Why so many batteries?

The rat seemed unconcerned. It continued to move towards the terminal, finally disappearing from Griggs' line of sight. For a moment, he was tempted to move closer to the edge, to follow the rat's path towards the safety of some crack in the cement. He could see himself stepping over the warning line, falling to his knees and leaning his head out over the edge as if it were a headman's block—watching the rodent crawl to safety, even as someone screamed and the purging roar of the train rose to a deafening crescendo.

But instead he just stood there. Watching.

The train pulled to a stop and he waited till the deluge of pedestrians flooded off, then slipped aboard himself. Twenty eight years of traveling the city's underground told him right where to go: to the rear corner of the car, to that compact little tramp's haven of four seats. He let himself collapse, sighed at the relief to his knees and back. The globular growths inside him settled into place.

The doors shut and the train began to move. He took another quick nip from the vodka bottle.

He thought of Gail and the kids—and, as the train jerked to life, he thought of a thousand different Gails, a thousand different Ambers and Keiths—should he feel worse for having left them? The three of them, after all, had just kind of showed up at different points in his life, unrequested but accepted marker points in what he'd always expected of a normal life. Gail had wanted to date him, so they'd dated. Gail had wanted to move in together, to marry, to have a kid and he'd agreed to all those bonds of normalcy,

Now they were severed from him. Where, in his current predicament, did he fit into their prime time TV world?

In the end, this was happening to him . . . He was the victim, the sufferer, the sad-fleshed vessel.

Things blurred further.

Rise.

He imagined a thousand burrow-ing tunnels . . .

Rise.

. . . a thousand frenzied eruptions . . .

Rise.

. . . a thousand brilliant, burning suns . . .

He forced himself to open his eyes and sit up a little, willed himself back out of the kaleidoscope. He mustn't give into it just yet, couldn't surrender before he knew.

To run was selfish, but what could a doctor have done? What would they do if he went to them now? Crush the growths one-by-one till the pain drove him mad? Slice him open and let this sad sack of skin fall like a bloody cloak from the bulk of his malignancy?

There was no going back.

Π

As the train moved from terminal to terminal, each jerking stop sent his mind reeling. He soon became unsure where they were in relation to the stretch of tunnel that had changed him. But when he was there, he'd know.

For a time, he drifted in and out of slumber, subdued by the booze in his system, by the whine of the train and the steady throttle of the tracks. The human cacophony of his fellow passengers was almost comforting.

He dreamt of a thousand Gails weeping in surgical wards—the doorways all strangely circular, the sterile hospital hallways beyond them curving upwards with the impossible angles of dreamscape architecture. He saw a thousand fetish models arching their backs for a photographer's ring flash, the gleam erasing the last symbol from each ceremonial blade. He felt the jar of subway cars jumping their tracks as the windows washed with black-green ink . . .

A sharp jolt woke him and he found the train still clicking along through the underground—except now it bore but two passengers: himself in his subway tramp's cubbyhole, and a thin, ragged-looking man halfway up the cab.

The stranger stood in the isle, one arm hanging from an overhead strap. He swayed too and fro with the rhythm of their movement, a constant sweep of long, greasy black hair and trailing raincoat.

Griggs stiffened, gripped his belly as a sharp pain thundered through his insides. He gritted his teeth to keep from calling out, closed his eyes.

He looked up and saw a jumble of gaunt strap-hangers turning around to stare at him—then just the one again.

Griggs gasped loudly, his eyes brimming with tears, but already the pain was fading into a web of pins and needles.

"You OK there, big fella?" The man asked. His beard was scraggly, his face emaciated. His wide, junkie eyes twitched with manic intensity.

"I'm fine." Griggs grunted, looking back down at the floor, trying to calm his breathing.

"You sure about that?"

The stranger was walking toward him now. Free of the strap, he moved slowly down the isle, swaying to either side with the movements of the train.

"I'm sure," Griggs grated, sterner this time.

"Really? You don't look so hot." The man stopped and braced himself against the subway bar just a few feet away. "Where ya headed, bro?"

"Home."

"That's where the heart is . . . "

"Please leave me alone."

"Hey, no problem . . . " The stranger smiled a yellow, toothy grin. "I don't mean to hassle. I just know—fuck man, riding these things can take a lot out of a fella."

"Look, I . . ."

"last time," the stranger said, "they had to cut me out with a torch —a fuck'n *torch*. Can you believe that?"

Griggs stared up to meet the stranger's eyes again. "You were there?"

"Two weeks ago," the stranger said. "We're close to it, you know. Get off at the next stop and I'll take you there.

"No . . . look, I don't know—"

"Yeah you do . . . " The man said, nodding matter-of-factly. "That stretch of tunnel ain't gonna be open again any time soon. They gotta *test*, gotta scrape, gotta find out what happened . . . kinda like you, right? Kinda like me. Can't say I blame ya for not really do'n all the math. Hell, I only know the score 'cause I've been riding these lines solid the last 48 hours. And I want the same thing you do."

Griggs looked up at the shabby stranger's face, stared deep into those addled, blood-shot eyes. His pupils were enormous.

The man cracked his black and yellow grin again. "Yeah, we got ourselves changed in different ways. Did you see it before it got to you? I'm guessing not, since it did you up the way it did."

The stranger pulled one arm from the sleeve of his raincoat, and then began untucking his black t-shirt.

"Me, I saw the fucker crash through the door," he said, "saw it right before it did me up with *this*."

He pulled the shirt up and exposed the right side of his torso. Scarlet veins visible under his pale skin, webbing out from the black, rotting wound his side. Griggs could plainly observe the ribs rising and falling with each breath, underneath the tight canvas of burned flesh.

"It stung me, I guess," he said, letting his shirt fall to conceal it again.

"Now, why ain't I dead, right?" he asked, gesturing wildly. "Why ain't my heart stopped cold with this shit? Why's it been like one long fucking meth bender since the wreck? I don't know . . . don't even know if there's really any percentage in asking. But then I started trying to wrap my head around the way it made me *feel*—and not just feel,

but *think*, ya know? Best I can figure, that thing came from someplace else, some place deep down . . . "

He trailed off, staring down wide eyed and twitching, as if he might, by sheer junkie will, see through the floor and into the bowels of the earth itself.

The train began to slow towards its next stop. The man shot his glance back to Griggs—put a hand on his shoulder.

"This is it," he said. "No or never."

Griggs stared out the window again, at the alternating stretches of solid concrete and hungry darkness. "Help me up," he said. "Help me walk."

Π

They disembarked at the next stop and the stranger, who finally introduced himself as Alan, picked the lock on an "authorized personnel only" door and led the way through a cluttered storage room, down a corridor, and out into the darkness of the subway tunnels.

They crept along the walkway, guided by the glow of Alan's flashlight. Griggs kept his back against the wall for support, kept one hand firmly on his guide's shoulder and side-shuffled his way down the tunnel. Their progress was slow and labored, but relentless.

In the dark, Griggs detected a slight glow emanating from Alan's neck. He soon realized it was where some of the blackened flesh crept above his shirt collar, the pulsing vein at its center burning with soft, scarlet luminosity. It brought to mind the things that lived in deep-sea trenches.

"The wreckage is still a good ways up ahead," Alan said. "But what we're looking for is going to show up a lot sooner."

Griggs' breathing became more and more labored, his knees and back throbbing from the weight of his burden. He also soon began to notice patches on the tunnel wall covered in dark slime. At one point, he nearly tripped over something large and wet on the narrow walkway—something that made a sound like rotten fruit as it tumbled down to the tracks below.

Panicked, he'd struggled for balance, started to lower himself down to the safet of a seated position—but Alan grabbed him under one arm and hauled him back to his feet.

"Not yet," the stranger grunted, "If you sit down, I might not be able to get you back up—and we're so close I can fucking *feel* it."

All Griggs could feel, however, was weariness—in his limbs, in his breathing, in every sad inch of his pathetic hide. His vision momentarily blurred when he looked at Alan's flashlight and he saw a thousand torch beams searing down a thousand tunnels.

And then he heard it.

They both recoiled, Alan jerking his head around to stare back down the way they'd traveled. The sound was unmistakable: not the movements of secret things in the dark, but the growing vibrations of an approaching subway car.

"Train . . . " Griggs said. "I thought the—"

"Come on!" Alan yelled, tugging him up by the arm. "We gotta get you into the next alcove!"

And he realized it was true—while his slender guide could, in theory, simply cling to the wall and let the train pass, Griggs' bulk was too much. A passing car was bound to rupture him, rip his belly open like a sack of garbage.

He thought again of the windows suddenly awash with dark green liquid, the sounds of movement on the roof.

"Move!" Alan screamed, grab-bing him by the shirt collar.

Griggs began to shamble at full speed behind him. How far back was the last alcove? What was their interval? He hadn't thought to notice or keep track. What if he wouldn't fit?

Soon, he'd feel the subterranean ozone wind rushing in approach of his death. By the time the lights were visible, it'd be too late.

He thought of the dancing paper, the rat squirming its way into some hidden hole.

Better to just fall in front of it, should it come to that, better to just have it all at once.

His breathing became a series of labored gasps, each racking his entire torso.

"I think there's one up here!" Alan screeched. "Just a little farther!"

But he could already feel the wind building up. His vision blurred out a little more with each struggled step and he felt his insides tremor.

Recklessly, he pushed himself harder. The ledge became slippery, his footing even more uncertain

"Here!" Alan cried. "Quick, get—"

He stopped and Griggs stumbled into him.

"What's wrong?" he cried between breathes, his voice probably too soft to be heard at all.

And then he saw it.

The stranger's flashlight beam illuminated a wall of black, rotting meat where his refuge should have been—every inch of the alcove packed solid with hewn slabs of flesh and the jutting remains of broken, crustacean-like appendages, each the size of a tree branches.

Oh god, oh god, oh god oh god

. . .

The wall leading on beyond was smeared solid with inky fluid.

Behind them, the roar grew louder.

Alan reached his arms into the rancid meat and pulled out one of the dripping, segmented appendages, let it tumble down to the tracks. Then another. In a frenzy, he grabbed hold of the edges of a chunk the size of a side of beef and began to tug on it, throwing all his weight into wrenching it from the clogged alcove, opening it like a slow-hinged doorway to a world of oily rot.

The lights of the approaching train began to glow behind them, casting their long, doomed shadows down the tunnel ahead. Griggs felt his bowls loosen, felt the hot trickle of urine down his leg.

Trembling uncontrollably, he made ready to let himself fall.

"Here!" Alan yelled, "Just enough room!"

Another slab of flesh finally came out, tumbled down wetly to the tracks.

Griggs felt himself pulled toward the meat-choked alcove, felt Alan viciously trying to shove him, back first, into the hole he'd dug out, wet and slick in the flashlight's glow. It smelled like rot smothered in incense, a great heap of spiced decay.

Cold, foul liquid poured over him as Alan pressed him into the spongy meat. More of it shifted, fell around him in ropey strings.

"You're almost there!" Alan screamed.

And then the light was upon them, blasting full force.

He heard the screech of breaks, felt his foot slipping against the edge of the walkway as Alan continued to push him in with a desperate cry.

Alan slipped and the two of them collapsed against the meat, their legs splaying out over the edge of the walkway. Griggs tried to scramble back up, but only slid a little further. He rolled onto his side and suddenly felt most of his belly hanging out in the train's path.

Gasping, he looked up and saw only blinding lightheard only the groan of metal.

And then the flashlight beam moved away from his face.

"It's him!" Boomed a voice.

A single open-platform maintenance car coasted to a stop just a little behind themnot the unstoppable bullet of a subway car, but something far smaller, far less sleek.

Griggs stared in numb disbelief.

Its bed was cluttered with green boxes and portable lighting, along with what looked like a small crane. Several men crouched here and there amid the clutter. Some were dressed in bright yellow rain coats, a couple of others seemed to be transit police.

Oh god . . .

Griggs fumbled in his pocket for the loose collection of sleeping pills. He wouldn't let them take him—not to some cell, not to some doctor's probing needles.

He pulled out a fistful.

Alan grabbed his hand. "No you don't!"

Most of them spilled from his fist in the struggle—the rest Alan forcibly tried to keep away from his face. Griggs looked up to see one of the men in the florescent rain coats jumping across the gap onto the walkway. He could already imagine the words: *"Mr. Griggs, your wife has been very worried about you . . . We have to get you to a doctor right away . . . This is a restricted area, we really . . . "*

"We have found you," said the man in the yellow coat, his face half lost to black skin and creeping red veins. His eyes, like Alan's, burned with manic intensity. "The One whose coming was foretold by the Great Mother's wound."

The man lifted the right side of his raincoat and revealed a dark, wet wound in his side, pulsing red veins fanning out around it through his torso.

At that, the other half-dozen men on the maintenance car unbuttoned their raincoats and pulled open their shirts. Each bore the same cancer-black puncture in their right side, pierced through the ribs like the work of some deranged Caravaggio. One man, standing towards the back, was almost completely charred from the venomhunched over, wheezing and twitch-ing, but eyeing Griggs with intense interest all the same.

"We'll take you the rest of the way down," the man in front said.

Griggs kept his fist tightly clenched. Alan kept his grip on the wrist. He didn't move—wasn't sure he could now that he was off his feet.

"Where?" He asked.

"To the Great Below," the man said. "The vent is just ahead"

A tremor moved through him again, his perspective shattered into a thousand separate streams before he felt his consciousness collapse back to its normal proportions.

Rise.

He swallowed, hard and dry.

Rise.

He opened his tightly clenched fist, revealed an empty palm.

"Oh god . . . " Alan moaned.

"How many?" the lead stranger asked.

Alan grabbed Griggs' jaw and pried it open. He felt the dirty, probing fingers fumbling around in his gums.

"Couldn't have been many," Alan said, "I'll gag him."

Griggs felt the fingers shoot to the back of his throat.

"No!" a raspy voice called out from the maintenance car, "Too risky . . . "

Alan pulled his fingers out and Griggs doubled over in coughs, in revulsion, but he didn't vomit. He felt the numbness inside him tremble, felt his consciousness swell again, but it held. He looked up to see the source of the raspy voice: the hunched-over man from the back of the cart, his head completely scourged and hairless from the poison coursing through him.

"We have to take him down now," the dark man continued. "It can't happen here . . . "

Somehow, they managed to get him to his feet. They seemed worried, but not irate. With the utmost care, they hefted him across the gap to their open-roofed vehicle. He managed to exert enough energy to keep from being complete dead weight, but the pills were already taking hold of him. They eased him to the floor beside a generator. One of them even gathered some coats and tarps for him to lay on.

Before the engine started again, Griggs noticed something shining in the meat still clogging the alcove, gleaming like a jewel set in black flesh.

It was a single, great eye.

Π

Between the roar of the engine and the drugs filtering through his system, he began to sleep—began to feel his consciousness drift apart into a thousand dream fragments, a thousand pieces that, together, formed a staggering mosaic.

He saw the Great Below the strangers had spoken of, saw the mind-numbing expanses of desert and strife, the fire storms and poisoned oceans that carved the inner hells.

Jungles of thorn and venom crowded the fore hills of jagged, black mountains. Volcanic peaks bled forth rivers of living sewage, the banks of which swarmed with mammoth, wingless birds. Their eyes were mounds of scar tissue, their flesh crawling with a tapestry of scabs and vermin. Occasionally, the great beasts wandered far enough from the banks to sniff out the mountain-bound slave caravans of chained, humanoid rabbits—and fell on them ravenously.

The slave drivers—squat and bundled from head to toe in crimson scarves—scurried for the cover of thorn trees as the birds fought one another over their leporid prey. They pecked at eyes long-lost to past scuffles, added further gashes to each other's ravaged, hoary heads. The chained, furry things at their feet merely shrieked in terror as they were gobbled whole.

When the most gluttonous bird had eaten its fill, its brothers fell to ripping at its bloated abdomen with greedy talons and hungry beaks. Streaked in bloody bowel, already searing with the agonies of near-digestion, the rabbit men's still-squirming bodies tumbled out onto the ground like dripping newborns, only to be gobbled up one again.

The wastes stretched on. Everywhere, there was strife, everywhere there was death.

He glimpsed where armies of vaguely anthropomorphic horrors lay in besiegement to a mountain fortress. The warriors' faces were consumed by enflamed flesh, lost to the twisted in-growth of their spiral horns, their bodies thickly muscled over twiste, elephant man skeletons. Wave after wave, they sacrificed themselves in great piles against the high walls of the fortress—falling to rains of arrows, burning pitch and worse.

Great rotting titans manned the towers high above, each bound by chains to their fortifications, where cloaked, man-sized beings prodded them to action with flaming tridents and spears. With each fiery wound to their flanks, one of the howling giants would plunge its claws into its own stomach and tear forth a squirming troll-child, then heave the dripping, thrashing mess down onto the besiegers like a boulder.

The ripped remnants of each titan's gut then sizzled and smoked with regeneration, till such time as the sinking of a flaming pike bid them plunge into their bodies once more for fodder.

And the sky above—if it were truly sky—burned with an unnatural amber-orange glow that made him think of rotting jungle flowers, the rancid sweetness of spoiled fruit.

Griggs heard again the voice of compulsion:

Rise.

He glimpsed the untold hordes rising up from even greater depths, out of the breathing tunnels that buried still deeper into greater planes of Boschian misery . . .

Rise.

. . . spiraling up from the very bottom of the universe . . .

Rise.

He saw the black legions swell, felt them wash over both the besiegers and fortress like a wave, over birds and prey, over canyons of blood and temples of bone.

Griggs' consciousness collapsed back on itself and he saw darkness again, felt the floor beneath him moving, felt himself swaying on some uneven platform. He opened his eyes to the flickering glow of electric lanterns reflected against a ceiling of wet, black rock.

Wrapped in bits of tarp and a few ragged winter coats, he was strapped securely to a makeshift litter built from pipes, aluminum sheeting and oily rope. The blackened men bore him, awkwardly navigating the oddly-hewn tunnel that twisted down at a steady rate of decent.

His bearers didn't say a word to him, slowed only as the difficulties of their path required. At one point, one of the men collapsed wheezing to the tunnel floor. Their progress stopped for but a second.

"Leave him," Alan said, "He has succumbed."

Π

Hours passed before they lowered the litter of pipes and rags to the ground, each of its five surviving bearers groaning with relief. Griggs, still wrapped in a pile of coats, looked uncertainly up at the great rock cavern surrounding them

The strangers cut loose his bonds and extinguished their flashlights, but he could still hear them near him, wheezing and struggling for breath in the dark.

Despite their hours of passage through the black tunnel, it was not the perfect dark of some subterranean cavern that surrounded them. The darkness seemed *wet* somehow, moist and glistening with the faintest scarlet illumination, clinging to the jagged rocks and vaulted ceiling far overhead. There was the faintest movement of air through the chamber—a horrible warm breeze that smelled of rot and fetid waters.

And there was something else here was well, something that called out to him wordlessly, stirred the vast numbness inside him.

His vision shifted to the perspective of legion again and he saw the great chamber illuminated in sparkling crimson. The strangers knelt to either side of him like royal subjects, the twisting black trails of their poison showing strongly on their arms and faces. Half of Alan's beard had fallen out, replaced by black ruin.

The strangers turned their bowed heads towards something ahead in the darkness.

Griggs followed their gaze and saw, at last, the instrument of his change, one of the beings whose movements he had surely heard on the roof of the subway car, whose sibling's torn carcass they'd found mashed by the train's velocity into the alcove. This was the one whose kiss had filled him with this strange purpose, whose sting had turned the strangers into obedient preparers of The Way.

The creature's form was roughly that of a gargantuan arachnid—its gleaming black carapace that of some unimaginable crustacean, as if born to inhabit oceans of boiling tar. The steam rising from its surface betrayed the epic heat of the biologic processes within. Its blood must boil, he realized, the thing's massive heart like that of a spitted pig, cooked until it furiously began to pump with the boiling juices of its own roasting.

It crouched not like a spider set to pounce, but as if lost to some form of Tantric meditation. Its two front pairs of legs crossed, the lacework of overlapping limbs creating the shape of a diamond. Its great head was bowed, its eyes closed. At first he took the being's mouth parts for a great beak, but quickly understood them to be more akin to the closed and coiled tentacles of a cuttlefish. They drifted and caressed each other ever so slightly, as if afloat in dreams.

Slowly, Griggs moved from the litter, struggling against the torment of his weight and girth. At first he crawled across the cold rock floor—the rough and ragged edges of the stone cutting into his palms—but at last he rose to one swollen knee. Then the other.

The great eyes opened—figure-eight pupils the color of amber, each afloat in a sea of crimson jelly.

Dear god, how they burned—burned with leagues of longing, ages of toil and conquest. These were the eyes of a god, he realized, the eyes of untold millennia rising up through the depths.

"You did not abandon them in vain," the being spoke into his mind, each word vibrating, trembling, in his consciousness. "Your wife and young were but a precursor to your one true mate, to the offspring you were meant to bear . . . "

He touched his stomach, felt the globs trembling inside him. His eyes brimmed with tears. "Why?"

"Why?" it echoed, "But you were suffering already, stagnant, empty, human . . . and now your suffering has meaning. Is this not what you have longed for?"

"No . . . " Griggs moaned.

"But I know that it is," the voice said.

Griggs felt consciousness waver. The being's eyes multiplied. "What are you?"

"I am the grasping claw of the nameless," it said. "I am the conqueror, eternally reaching up towards the cosmos. For each world below that has fallen to me, each layer in the endless onion of existence, I have had absorb something of its denizens. To conquer, I must, in part, become. Your sun would destroy me as I am now . . . "

Through those thousand eyes, Griggs again glimpsed the crawling armies of arachnid horrors sweeping over the hell-ish worlds of pain, saw empires and demigods fall to their ravenous hunger.

Rise.

The consciousness of the conqueror entombed in all of them.

Rise.

A collective mind reaching for the stars.

Rise.

He felt the numbness stir.

"You will become a part of me," it said. "But you have already felt yourself awakening into it, haven't you?"

"I don't . . . "

"We are already becoming one . . . "

"I can't . . . "

"But you can," it whispered, "Taste my flesh. Let our vessels become fodder; let the progeny consume us both . . ."

Nathan Griggs heard the movement of the thing's other bodies in the darkness around him, moving with the stealthy swiftness of creeping shadows first dozens, but then hundreds. He starred deep into the creature's lustrous pupils. He felt the globs inside him vibrate, strained to stave off a desire to do the unthinkable.

Rise.

His hand burned as he thrust it into thing's eye, flesh bubbling and smoking. He screamed, but somehow brought the searing handful of jelly to his mouth.

Rise.

His face blacked, his eyes burst and his hair was singed back to blistered scalp. He fell backwards through the kaleidoscope again, tasting only pain.

Rise.

He felt the dark consciousness of the conqueror flowing into his mind.

Rise.

He felt the numbness shift, the walls of pathetic flesh rupturing and falling down all around him. He felt himself emerging through a thousand openings, even as he felt himself falling apart.

II

On the surface world above, the sun shone down through the prismatic gleam of skyscrapers, reflected a thousand ways off the great, sky-grasping glass and steelwork claws of the city.

Nathan Griggs emerged from the subway tunnel—a new man, a slim man, a stranger among strangers. A faint glow lingered in his eyes. He wore a yellow rain coat over an ill-fitting uniform.

"Excuse me . . . " he put a hand on the shoulder of the man in a nearby line.

The bearded Taxi driver turned around, irritation smeared across his face. "I'm just grabbing a coffee, pal, I'm—"

Griggs moved his palm to the side of the cabbie's ribcage. One quick jolt and the man doubled over on the sidewalk.

"I need a driver for the day, do you think you can manage?" he asked.

The sharp, black appendage dripped but a single droplet onto the pavement before withdrawing back through the seamless lips in Griggs' palm.

"Yes," the taxi driver said, eyes trembling as he looked back up at his master.

Twitching with frantic energy, the driver took him to a cheap hotel, the one he'd checked out of just 24 hours ago, in his old life.

He strolled effortlessly through the lobby, no longer burdened by his form, now finally at one with the legion of other selves he felt teaming in the tunnels below, pulling scraps of clothing from cancer-black corpses.

One mind. One hunger.

He took the elevator to the third floor, strolled carefully, silently down the hall to room 308—the place he'd fled to when the worst of it had taken hold of him. A "do not disturb" sign still hung on the doorknob.

He placed his palm on the door, felt the still coldness.

He tilted his head and moved his ear closer, heard the murmur of a television set from the other side. He fancied he could glimpse a hint of the pulsating light creeping out from underneath the door and shivered.

He jerked his hand away from the wood grain, the chill lingering in his fingertips.

"What pain is this?"

He heard the TV murmur from the other side grow louder: newscasts and Bugs Bunny, evangelism and whipping static, voices and splintering wood..

"Where am I?"

Gloomy Countdowns

by
William Doreski

Restoring The Sacred Dramas

In the world's most famous cathedral

we're replacing stained glass windows

with two-way LCDs wired

for digital bible dramas.

In the nave a big screen depicts

Cain's murder of Abel, the gush

of crimson from the clubbed skull

glib as a sunset. The next scene

features Eve caressing a snake,

the creature nuzzling her breasts

with shivers of requited pleasure.

Across the aisle the story

of Ruth gains zest by adding

a Mongol horde to rape her

again and again as the hushed

congregation enjoys itself

despite the trembling of the priest

before the Eucharist mystery.

As we proceed up the aisle

the stories become more livid:

Ezekiel munching scorpions;

Isaiah bulldozing fortresses;

Amos tossing a hand grenade

in Nebuchadnezzar's dining hall.

The apse offers milder fare:

Jesus bathing in the Sea

of Galilee, his manly torso

a pink confection; Simon Peter

hauling in a netful of sharks;

the Last Supper being served

by a bevy of adolescent

beauties with Pepsodent smiles.

The transept features Apocalypse:

horsemen tramping young mothers

pushing strollers; disease eating

the features of famous statesmen;

fire curdling Paris and New York.

The cathedral's electric bill

may bankrupt the diocese

but it's worth it, the writhing

of all this religion so vivid

people will return to church in droves,

saving their souls and exciting

senses they hadn't realized

were as spiritual as dogmas

yet so much simpler to believe.

*

The Usual Kind Of Apocalypse

 woman crouched at the telephone,

talking with hammerheaded glee.

She and I were struck by lightning

in a peculiar winter storm.

Entire villages collapsed

in the ice-fall, while the lightning

killed people using computers

or sprawled before the TV

chortling at dullish comedies.

She and I survived the blast,

but the fire destroyed the business

we'd struggled two decades to build.

Rare books. Hundreds of rare books,

ten million dollar inventory,

gone in a whisper of ash.

One book contained a signature

some scholars thought was Shakespeare's.

Now, after dreaming that storm,

I've awakened with the dark speared

through my heart, and that woman,

whose name eludes me, phoning

some lover to gloat that I'm dead.

Did we actually deal in books

together? What about Shakespeare,

who predicted this situation

except for the use of the phone?

She hangs up, looks so hard at me

I feel the stake twist and I cough

a gout of starlight and free myself.

We face each other. I almost

know her name, almost recall

that in some previous life

we had something human to share.

I realize her hands are gray

with ash. Tears muddle down her cheeks.

Frustration, of course, not sentiment.

Why won't I stay dead? A pink

unwholesome dawn occurs. The house,

I realize, is black with fire

and the outdoors shivers with ice

glazed a foot thick on everything.

I can thrust my arm through the hole

in my chest, a bloodless wound

that must've happened long ago

when the world we made was young

and the books we collected to sell

came cheaply, and I knew her name

as well as I know Shakespeare's,

one I would never take in vain.

*

🐸 Saint

Televised, a saint explodes

into light, his soul atomic,

extruded to fill the cosmos.

I watch the way a lizard watches

the sun crawl across the sky-dome.

Lacking religion, I assume

that special effects specialists

have devised this apocalypse

to befuddle the rubes who vote

while ankle-deep in manure.

But half of America's groaning

over its sins, while the other half

should be. The wind picks up not

like a dirge but a war cry,

ancient Achaean. A clatter

of arms, a rumble of bodies

falling in half-naked glory.

The saint reappears, smiling.

The audience can see he's whole,

self-resurrected. The light,

which for a moment I mistook

for oxygen deprivation,

has faded, leaving a person

as curly-haired and pout-lipped

as a Burberry model. He sways

on his elegant stem and describes

his visit with Jesus. Ten million

viewers kneel and weep. I switch

the TV to Monday Night Football,

but it's not even Monday night.

The groans of some foolish drama

depress me more than the saint did,

so I shut off the TV and lie

perfectly flat in bed and feel

how alone the universe is

with itself, how sadly it coughs up

novas, supernovas, black holes,

how crudely the great nebulae

sculpt themselves in the vacuum,

ghostly shapes too huge to imagine,

too star-spangled to deny.

✱

Numbers On The Night Sky

What are those huge glowing numbers

projected onto the night?

We stand in the pasture staring,

hoping to spot a falling star,

but enormous blocky numerals

flush the sky so brilliantly only

the boldest meteor would show.

Maybe a massive equation

is forming of its own volition,

preparing to solve a problem

unknown to the corporate world.

Maybe the solution has nothing

to do with dividends or profits

for CEOs and directors,

but derives from al that logic

orphaned when Professor Quine died.

We hug so firmly our bones creak,

so fearing permanent damage

to our psyches return to the house

and turn on every light to occlude

those terrible sizzling digits.

Maybe watching TV will numb us

to the crush of economics,

but we hear six hundred miles way

mountaintops exploding, debris

choking and poisoning rivers,

citizens huddling in the downdraft

collapsing wooden hamlets.

How can we sleep with those numbers

unexplained? We phone the police,

but they're frightened and ignorant,

so we scour the Internet and find

apocalypse routinized

and welcomed. We pull down the shades

and hope those numbers don't refer

to and don't include us. The night

sighs as snow-clouds arrive, snuffing

those enormous smoky figures

but leaving us wondering

what gloomy countdowns have begun.

*

Apothecary Hall

Where the abandoned railroad curves

past Apothecary Hall I watch

a groundhog stumble over rough ground,

his bulk impractical but cunning.

The fertilizer plant still functions,

but the name "Apothecary Hall"

no longer applies, replaced by

a big-time chemical name brand.

Forty years ago, my mother noticed

signs pointing to this landmark,

so we detoured only to find

a black factory brimming

with bleak organic smells. Now
trailer trucks crowd the loading dock
and an air of insolence smirks
above the scene. The groundhog leers

over his shoulder. The sky dims
to mock my lack of apocalypse.
Yet surely it will happen here,
if anywhere, the boiled light bubbling

with gestures, the woods on fire.
Here in Broad Brook, Connecticut,
the flowering of prophecies,
as Thomas Hooker saw, will happen

regardless of the tobacco fields
already planted, the long sheds
patient and slat-ribbed, the tractors
gnashing along dusty field-roads.

It will happen because long ago
dark satanic mills erupted
and a fertilizer plant named
Apothecary Hall disgusted

my mother, who'd expected
"something nice." It will happen

mainly because the world's bored,

sore heavy bored, and no one

will spike a prayer to stop it,

surrendering all flesh and matter

to the great singular organ

that will focus us forever.

*

Hard Landscapes

by
PJ Nolan

Dispatches

This morning, the patio is a chessboard

Drained of fight, a low contrast

Truce of gritty concrete squares

Slick under furniture pieces disarrayed;

Mouldering victims of a thuggish midnight squall.

Brick red when first assembled, inclemency

Has shrunk their ersatz teak to oldbone grey.

I know they've reached the rotting stage;

The last time they were used, not one

But two seats rent that sunny afternoon,

Their rundles detonating under laden

Celtic Tiger arses, ambushed.

Pig-in-the-parlour

I get up early and go down to the back garden.

A pinprick of purplish light expands to

A glowing fireball of foreboding in my forehead.

The temperature at its core is 50 million degrees centigrade.

I am still achingly sore.

Plenty, followed by famine, jostles

And hands the old bull over.

I put it on. I am 24 going on 14.

Discovering awful strength,

I lurch upwards ten feet.

Man's role is to start a new adventure

With enigmas - which is one reason I would break

Every rule in tomorrow's game.

Clock

Luna looming,

Ashveiled, mushrooming towards

Operatic advocacy.

Doors open.

Streetlights footlight,

Mountains edge the night.

Towns grow amber, mirroring

Cold cambers to stage

Where this story is played out.

Comes the chorus, addled,

Streaming roachcrazy

Via vomitoria.

Tidal pulling

Recedes, beaching unlulling words,

Silting a ghettotipped libretto

Unwritten, unlighting faces back

To shade.

The Tiles

The tiles

Are mosaic,

Buckled grids

Of commandment.

The tiles

Are choral,

Piping echoes

Clearing throat.

The tiles

Are martial,

Tightlipped

Pending battle cry.

The tiles

Are mute.

The Pippet's Nest

Summer before last,

When walking the old leadmine route,

Up from the smelter site below,

Alongside the granite and brickbuilt chimney

Laid above ground to the docked and isolated

Summit flue, I drifted from my group

To where the hillside had just recently burnt over.

There, like an open-air museum exhibit,

A nest lay on the ground, preserved

Intact, just toasted slightly on its fringes

Where the groundfire had buzzed over.

Meadow Pippet, surely, was the informed answer

To my query afterwards.

I still have the photograph I took,

Amazed that gorze and grasses were sheared bare,

But this wee birdy homestead was preserved.

But, truly, as a home did it survive?

For in the nest were three small eggs,

Deserted and long dead, I guessed at first.

I couldn't help but wonder did they bake?

Were they hardboiled, inside their pale flecked shells

(And if so, might I have snacked that day?)

Or could it be those eggs were still alive?

Surviving then to grow and hatch under a parent

Returned after that local holocaust, not even fully cogniscent

Of their familial luck. Knowing that the air had changed,

But that their future still held better odds

For this choice of site - the place and time of their laying.

As months passed and I still did not return there, I wondered

If this fresh beginning was in fact the story's end? I hoped it was.

A crackle of some kind of hope in the flames of history.

But surely, lurking reason then declared, those bullet eggs were dead.

Long since broken down by nature's process, perhaps

Aided by some other, more thorough scavenger than I?

Or could it be they lie there still? Hard and shelled,

A camouflaged memorial in the matted autumn undergrowth.

Hidden, like that scattered shot of reddened lead

Now sown beneath Europe's napoleonic fields,

Once empirically gleaned from colonial Ireland's ore

And grown for battle seed in the flames of Ballycorus.

Church Of The Bitter Ray Gun

by Deb Hoag

We started out as two separate congregations: The Temple of the Just Desserts, and the Church of Books on Tape. But when part of the ceiling collapsed, killing Torte and leaving both chambers filled with debris and difficult to navigate, we had little choice but to leave the lofty heights of the Sales on Four Floor. After consultation with an initiate from the Shrine of the Handyman's Special, I ordered that we combine and look for a new church. We had little choice but to move deeper into the bowels of the building where the mutated kudzoo vine discouraged earlier settlers from finding sanctuary.

It was Tiramisu that uncovered the sign "B TTER RAY GUNS". She looked at me uncertainly. Macheted kudzoo lay around her up to her knees. "What does this mean, Oh Lord of the R—"

Before she could finish her question, there was a blinding flash of purple light. For a moment, lurid spots danced in front of my eyes, and I had to shake my head to clear my vision.

The sight I beheld made me wish I could still not see. Mousse, husband of Tiramisu, had been examining one of the ray guns from the glass cases all around us, and while looking, had apparently thumbed the trigger just enough to sear off most of his left hand.

His severed fingers twitched on the floor, even as he gaped at the stumps on his hand. Then he looked up, smiled weakly and passed out cold.

Hannibal picked Mousse up and placed him on top of one of the clear cases, while I gingerly picked up the discarded ray gun and put it out of harm's way on a high shelf. We clustered around, studying his left hand. "At least, the ray seems to have cauterized the wound," said Hyperion.

I concurred. "Harrys?" Several Potterites answered as one. This really used to bother me, but once I accepted the idea that the Harrys are going to stick together no matter what, I was able to move past my frustration and concentrate on assigning them tasks that take a whole group to do. "Listen you guys—and gal—I want you to hop up to the Cathedral of Electronics and see it they have something that can fix Mousse up, somehow. 'Cause there's no way we're going to get those fingers re-attached."

As a unit, the Harrys turned to go, although the Harry-Book Five gave me a suspicious, angry grimace before taking off.

The High Priest of Electronics, Duracell, had something he thought might do the trick, and sent back a robotically controlled hand. We were able to modify the robotic hand and get the contraption attached to Mousse without having to detach any more of his real fingers.

Once Mousse was settled, we hunkered down to review our situation. Which was, basically, not good, but substantially improved over what our situation had been just that morning, when we had no weapons, no idea where we were going, and nothing to barter with.

We discussed the pros and cons of staying here and becoming the Church of the Bitter Ray Gun. Tiramisu and Éclair were both a little nervous about staying in a place that had weapons, but they had to admit that if we didn't stay, it was only a matter of time before someone else came down here and founded a church. And they might not like us.

Mousse finally settled matters by lurching to his feet and announcing his decision. "I am staying," he announced. "And I am taking a new name." We waited politely for a moment, giving him time to gather his thoughts.

When he did not proceed, I gave him a prompt. "Mousse, will you tell us the new name you have chosen?"

He raised his half-human, half-metal hand and waved it back and forth. The metallic fingers caught the light. "Semi Automatic."

Of course, once Mousse had made up *his* mind, Tiramisu let him make up *her* mind, too. And where Tiramisu goes, Éclair follows. Éclair can really be a cream puff sometimes. I could understand, to a degree—Tiramisu *was* the only one of us that knows anything about child birth. After all, Éclair did have a bun in the oven. When Éclair and Tiramisu ganged up like this, everyone else pretty much went along. They were the only two women in our group, aside from a half-grown Harry that none of us knew quite what to make of. I may have a small plot to hoe, but it's a lively one.

"Well, it's decided, then. I now christen this habitat the Church of the Bitter Raygun." We all solemnly spit in our respective palms and did high-fives all around.

#

Slowly, we all settled in and chose names for ourselves, while I worked on the liturgy for our new church. The chubbiest Harry became Cathode, followed by Heat, Shrink, Death and Freeze. As leader, I was quickly dubbed MasterBlaster. The charming Tiramisu became Stun, and Éclair, looking as if she could give birth any minute, became Fully Loaded.

One day, as we were lazing about, enjoying the fruits of our labors, Boom Box, one of the altar boys from the Church of Electronics, came zipping into our midst. He and the Rays (formerly the Harrys) had grown up together, and we maintained fond ties, even though we were now on different floors. "MasterBlaster, I have news. Duracell has bid me come and warn you that the Deacons of BodyBuilders of Powerhouse covet your new Church, and are plotting to take it from you. They have already begun taking the holy Steroid Wafers in preparation for their Assault!"

This should not have come as much of a surprise, but it did. We all knew that the zealot Deacons of Powerhouse were uneasily positioned between the Monks of the Secrets of Victoria, and the Sisters of the Congregation of Curves.

They were all uneasy neighbors at best, and the Berserker Deacons were known for taking what was not freely given to them.

My congregation drew near to me, beseeching me to tell them what to do. "My brothers and sisters, we know the burden we bear. Does not the title of our church tell us that a bitter lot shall be ours for worshiping the Holy Ray Gun? Now we must gather our weapons to us, and prepare to use them against all who would attack! Never must the Church of the Bitter Ray Gun be overrun by infidels! Are you with me?"

To my immense pleasure, the small crowd cheered and whistled and stomped their feet with enthusiasm. There was a wave of sound that washed over us as every gun was drawn and taken off "safety". A steady chant of "Death Ray, Death Ray, Death Ray!" created a solid wall of sound to repel our enemies.

Not a moment too soon. The Deacons of Powerhouse came rappelling down from the balconies of Sales on Four Floor, and, landing lightly on their muscular feet, stood before us in various threatening and statuesque poses. I glanced at my congregation gathered behind me, and raised my GalaxyBlaster Special.

The High Priest of Powerhouse sneered and flexed his glistening biceps. "Your puny weapons do not frighten us! We have muscle and extreme good looks on our side!"

I pressed the discharge trigger on my GalaxyBlaster, and a beam of blue light shot out, neatly severing a huge swatch of kudzoo, which fell at the feet of the Deacons of Powerhouse. The High Priest looked at the severed vines piled up at his feet, and then at the balcony, a good twenty feet overhead, from whence they had come. "Well," he said, squinting back and forth.

"Indeed," I replied.

"MasterBlaster?" said Stun from my left.

"I'm a little busy at the moment, dear," I muttered out of the side of my mouth. The High Priest was consulting with his followers, who were still looking back and forth from the severed vines to the spot they had fallen from.

"But, MasterBlaster, look!" I turned to look at Stun, and then followed the direction of her upraised arm. Where the kudzoo vines had fallen, now was revealed another, larger sign that announced our church far and wide for all to see. But it was not the church of the *Bitter* Ray Gun, as we had all supposed. Instead, in apple-red block letters, the sign proclaimed for all to see, "BETTER RAY GUNS". Better Ray Guns? *Better* Ray Guns? What could this portend? Instead of world-weary, cynical outcasts, as we had supposed, our calling was to be *better*? Better what? Dancers? Human beings? Bowlers?

An unearthly feeling crept up my spine as I stood, gaping at this revelation. I wrenched my eyes away with difficulty to those waiting, gathered around me. The Deacons of Powerhouse had already begun to slink away in retreat. I rushed up to their High Priest before he could escape, and threw my arms around him in friendship. "Brother!"

"Grumphigle?" He wheezed out. I loosened by grip, and he drew in a breath. "Brother?"

"Do you not see?" I exclaimed, overcome with righteous zeal.

"We are the Church of the Better Ray Gun. How shall we be better, but to put all this strife aside and become brothers to all those of the Discount Shop 'Til You Drop Mall? We are truly one mansion with many rooms, and all well furnished in our respective styles at the final hour. Does this not explain why all our many houses of worship are featured equally in the Fall Catalog? Can you not see?"

The High Priest looked at me thoughtfully. Already, I could tell the Berserker rage was subsiding in his visage. "Then all under this roof are of one family, despite our differences? What about the Bargain Basement Indoor/Outdoor Furniture and Garden Accents Gang?"

That was a tough call. I could see several of the Patty O' gnomes peering at us from under cover of the heavy kudzoo. They wouldn't take sides in a battle, of course, but they were poised and ready to scavenge the battlefield after the fact. One could hardly blame them, so little and spindly. They were also suspected of slinking about our churches when all were sleeping, and pilfering whatever was not guarded—unmated socks, safety pins, Raid.

"Everyone wants a sturdy and durable garden entertainment center to give their home that special touch, don't they?" I asked. The Patty O' gnomes cheered lustily. Some of them actually left their hiding places amidst the kudzoo to give me a standing ovation. I beamed at them.

"All!" I said firmly, draping one arm around his shoulder as we turned to face the gathered crowd. From hiding places all around, the Sisters of Curves and the Monks of the Secrets of Victoria began to emerge, and embrace the congregation of the Powerhouse and the Church of the Better Ray Gun. I beamed down on them beneficently. My people, my family.

From behind me I heard a small moan. Stun stood by Fully Loaded, who was grimacing in pain. Her eyes were wide as they sought mine. "It's the baby, MasterBlaster! It comes now!"

I turned back to the hugging, milling crowd. "Quick," I shouted. "Is there a healer from the Shrine of Dr. Soles in the house?"

'Bitter Ray Gun' by John Lee

'Industrial Waste' by Dave Migm

'How Will it End' by Steven Archer

'L'ange Noir' by Dave Migman

'Lady of Fire' by Steven Archer

'Cult' by Dave Migman

'Apocalypses & Garden Furniture' by John Lee

'Crakd Eye' by Dave Migman

'Lord of the Dance'
by Dave Migman

'Nu-cklear' by Dave Migman

'Oblivious Tea Drinkers' by Flavia Lytle

'Portrait of a Mad Thing' by Dave Migma

'Vampire Gal' by Dave Migman

'Ribbons' by Steven Archer

'SteamPunk Angel' by Malcolm McClinton

'Zombie Love Song' by Malcolm McClinton

Zombie Love Song

**by
Adam Lowe**

She smelled of shit and she was beautiful. It was on a waste heap outside Calcutta that Mother Earth regurgitated her. Jamie was human no more.

I saw her blood filter amongst rotting food and ash; I saw vines ravelling over her body. Then she rose, an animated corpse, with flies and stench billowing from her bloated lips. Maggots fell from her vagina, her nose. Compost steam wafted from her gold skin.

And she smiled at me. I knew she remembered. Death couldn't steal that. She was a chthonic queen, resurrected by the angry soil and the screaming wind. Green shoots pricked up through her epidermis and flowered into lilies across her arms. Then, just as quickly, they withered and died, falling away and leaving weeping holes behind.

Across the world, her subjects were summoned from their resting places, sprouting up in waves with her as the epicentre. Vindication of my love, you might say. Corpses crawled from wells in Jordan, bodies slithered from Popish catacombs, and the dead swam out of swamps in New Orleans. Her armies formed in a matter of days. The news presenters called it a revelation of chaos; the scientists called it a monstrous disease. I called it a challenge, and I called her Love.

I was a scientist. To leave her to fate was to deny my education.

We were here to study the viral strain of mutant plants overtaking the country. We were collecting samples from the tips and slums when she breathed lethal spores into her lungs and collapsed. I knew the symptoms: exploded lungs; fungal infestation of the respiratory system; algae in the blood. Death was an obvious side effect.

Taking off my lab coat, I wrapped her in it, bundled her into my wheelbarrow and set off for the lab. There must be a way to save her. She was alive. Perhaps the spores were yet to settle into her alveoli and the virus was yet to spread.

The lab was half a mile away, so I had to negotiate the rowdy streets with a writhing woman thrashing in my wheelbarrow and a thumping, heat-induced headache testing my patience.

'Arranged marriage,' I said with a hasty smile to a kid selling tea in cracked mugs. I don't think he understood me or cared. Calcutta's like that.

I dodged bicycles and rickshaws, bowled over an elderly woman as I ran, and dropped my glasses amongst the bustle of a fish market. After rushing into the lab, I cleared a table of the plant pots and flowers we were studying and delicately placed Jamie down. She stared at the ceiling, dazed, mouthing something I couldn't understand. My immediate concern was to take blood samples, mouth swabs, temperature readings. This must be some tropical virus, I reasoned. She was infected and didn't die, as I thought, but fell into a deep coma which she was now returning from.

Her temperature was nearly fifty degrees centigrade. At the micro level, her cells grew, died and replenished at an accelerated rate. When she finally regained consciousness, her functioning was unimpaired.

'Jamie.'

'Dr Stanford,' she said, a savage gleam in her eyes.

She never called me Dr Stanford. She always called me Aaron, or Aar. Gone were her smiles and coy glances.

'How are you feeling?' I asked.

'Alive. Burning with life.'

'You have a fever.'

'I have to leave, Dr Stanford.' She sat up on the examination table, regarding the mutant flora scattered across the floor. For a moment, she appeared to stiffen. Then she relaxed again and swung her feet over the table edge.

'Please . . . you can't. Not yet. You're very, very sick. I have to find out what's wrong with you. We have to wait for the toxicology analysis of your blood. I haven't had time—'

'Dr Stanford, I must go.'

I shook my head. 'You can't.'

Silence crystallised between us. The wildness was gone from her eyes and I could see pain there instead.

'Aaron.' She paused, taking her eyes off me. 'This isn't a virus. This is beyond science—above it. You can't fix this.'

'But let me try.'

'I have a task.' She walked towards the door and I blocked her exit with my body. 'Dr Stanford, I'm serious.'

'Give me a week.'

She examined me carefully. We both knew I could overpower her and keep her locked in here with me.

'If you fail to find a "cure",' she began, pouring scorn upon the idea, 'I will kill you. And in the meantime, if you are to have unfettered access to my body, I will have control of yours.'

I nodded. 'But you must allow me to continue my research into your condition.'

And so it began. I locked us in and welded the doors shut.

I examined her hair. Trace elements of sulphur, calcium and radon.

She shaved my head and carved flowers into my scalp.

I examined her faeces. It was infested with worms and covered with moss. When used as a fertiliser, it stimulated sudden growth, then swift decay in any plant I tried.

Jamie smiled as she reached into my own anus and pulled stinking fistfuls from inside. These she styled into a small scat ziggurat over which she squatted, watering it with her menses. She kissed this rank golem, encouraging a sunflower to grow from its summit.

In my haste, I had failed to check there were ample food supplies for two. Jamie smiled, fruit flies crawling over her sticky lips, and force fed me her exotic excretions. It was loaded with seeds and tasted of anise. Though my first attempt to swallow brought a fit of retching, she soon had me devouring the funky banquet to satisfy my hunger. Better still, it was self-replenishing and sprouted everything from daisies to roses. Each night we dined on petals and shit. It was a fitting symbol for our love.

I examined her mucous. Enzymes were present that instigated rapid healing. But it also became acidic upon exposure to light and corroded beakers and wood.

She took traces of this paradox ichor and swished it round my lips. My mouth then burned and bled, until she lapped, dog-like, at my injuries and watched them heal. This was the nearest I got to a kiss, and despite my pain, I quivered at the stroke of her tongue.

Finally, after my options were exhausted and I began to panic, she grew frustrated with my angst and beat me to the floor with her bare hands. Four of my ribs were broken.

She was impatient with my misery. It was not enough that I loved her so much I sought answers. It was not enough that I gave her command of my body. I might lose her after all, if she was even the same person as before. Though she looked the same, there was something dark and primal within her; something fierce and terrible. I overlooked the transformations occurring within.

In our isolation, I also failed to account for Jamie's hellish hordes. These zombie brethren were ravenous, carnal ghouls. They swarmed cities, overrunning all with rats, lice, dandelions, snakes and opium poppies. Flickering radio reports provided stuttered warnings through bursts of static. Hundreds of her footsoldiers made thousands more by biting and fucking the healthy. Soon swathes of them scoured the planet, smashing buildings and churning out streams of human waste across the landscape. My Jamie was only the first of many.

'It's the last day,' she said when my time came.

I knew I had failed. Science faltered at her biology; nature turned against me. This beast couldn't be the Jamie I knew. There were only two solutions: my death or my transformation.

Hungry demons began to bray against the roof and walls of the lab. The din was awful and my gut tightened. Maybe death had taken love from me after all?

'Have you cured me?'

'I . . . I . . . ' I longed for her. I did. I so wanted to save her, to be with her. And yet, she confounded me. All my inquiries and my learning meant nothing. She was a loathsome confection. She was treacle laden with glass.

'I . . . ' But I couldn't finish. The

walls burst in on us and her armies enfolded me. Ragged teeth and thorny pricks penetrated my soft, raw meat. They gnawed and sucked and slurped.

I was zombie food.

∏

After they chewed me up and spat me out, Jamie collected me together and made me her king. Our children covered the world in stinking fecundity. Carpets of compost, rivers of waste and seas of rot. The planet warmed up.

Then it began to change. Just a little, at first: a ripple of trees erupted in Paris. Then a wave, then a great seething tide of rebirth. Forests sprouted and then collapsed to mulch. A new, exaggerated cycle of life was beginning. Jamie and I presided over it all, atop a mountain of garbage. Flowers and sewage perfumed the air; toxic jungles rose from the cess.

When we felt our work was done, as a race we all turned to the blooming filth and crawled inside, nesting and cocooning in its foul warmth. Here, roots entangle us, burrowing creatures gnaw at our flesh and we gradually, as one, are beginning to dissolve into the compost forever.

Our armies are one with the peat. My limbs have already melted to mulch.

Tomorrow we will be gone.

Love And Gasoline

by
Michael R. Colangelo

Dear Journal:

This is how I meet (and lose) Jan.

It's my last year of high school.

They don't tell anyone. They're already out of the country, safely tucked away on some Pacific Island with the rest of the world's leaders.

I'm in the thick of the 2010 Civic Capital Riots with my brother, Bill.

We've tricked out Mom's old station wagon with steel-plate sidings. We've cut a murder hole out the rear window. It spits homemade napalm if anyone gets too close.

We're cruising towards Down-town to see if we can get in on any of the looting going on.

Instead, we're stuck in the middle of the riots. Bill literally turns the corner and we're caught between a group of students from the University on one side, and the tattered remnants of the 104th precinct on the other.

Things degenerate pretty quickly from here.

The cops—they've got a working riot gun with them. That by itself beats two hundred angry students any day of the week.

The students think they might like to flip Mom's wagon and use it as a defensive barricade. I spray them with the napalm gun to keep them off the car until the eventual smells of burning flesh and hair make me sick and I have to switch spots with Bill.

I roll the window down to breath, just a crack, trying to catch a breath. This girl comes running out of the mob with a riot baton and cracks it across the tips of my fingers. They are the only parts of me sticking out of the car.

Bill's got a homemade harpoon gun that fires lawn darts. He built it out in the garage over the week leading up to the chaos. I don't think his eyes ever left the CNN broadcast on the old black and white television out there.

Bill's good like that. He's paranoid to the core and used to be a real pain in the ass before all of this, but God if I don't love him for it right now.

Anyway—the gun is a real kick.

Remember those childhood warnings about throwing lawn darts at your cousins? Well, Jesus, if they weren't true. The darts made a mess. They broke bones and made an awful sound going in. Usually, if you fired the gun into a group, you'd only need to

POLLUTO.

hit one guy to make the others run in the opposite direction. They'd be cowed by the sheer violence of it all.

Bill's harpoon gun was totally sweet.

Right—so the second the baton comes crashing down on my fingertips, cracking the window beneath them, my other hand goes beside me and hefts Bill's gun.

I push it through the crack and level it at this girl. She's too busy staring at my shattered fingers to move in time and I'm about to pull the cord and let the lawn dart fly …

And then I hesitate.

She gasps and her whole chest heaves a little, and, well, it's pretty sexy.

She's got short blonde hair—a page haircut the fags call it. I guess the rape gangs might mistake her for a boy from a distance and leave her alone.

Anyways, short hair on chicks always does it for me -- even standing at the brink of the end of the world.

Instead of shooting her, I put the gun down and swing the door open.

Bill is all yelling from the back of the car, but he's too busy with his flame throwing to do anything about it.

"Get in! Let's get out of here!"

I'm screaming from the bottom of my heart.

She looks a little stunned by my proposal; a bit sheepish for breaking my hand. She chews on her lip and plays with the baton with her hands.

"Get in!" I repeat.

And to my amazement, it works.

With a quick glance around at the slaughter of her peers (the 104th precinct wins this one pretty handedly), she crawls across my lap and sits in the passenger seat.

I slam the car door shut and get the window up before any of her comrades can get close enough to drag me from the car.

Bill arcs the flamethrower at the ones that come close.

I'm backing the car over the bodies in the street when she introduces herself.

"Alex." I tell her. "That's Bill in the back."

"Nice to meet you."

Bill grunts a hello.

We give up on the organized looting and drive back towards the suburbs. She talks about her parents and what she used to do. I speak of the car and the intricacies of building a homemade flame-thrower. Bill complains that there isn't enough food for a third, how he hadn't planned for this, and how we're probably all fucked now.

She rolls her eyes playfully every time negativity comes drudging forth from the depths of the back seat, and I laugh.

She makes me laugh and I realize it's the first time I've done so since Doomsday.

We make love for the first time that night.

Okay. We fuck.

We have nasty sex in Bill's filthy basement washroom—the one with the exploded toilet with the dried piss and shit on the floor and walls. It's the only place private enough.

We don't talk about marriage or going steady or any of that. We don't share a cigarette afterwards. All the idealism is gone. Only the fucking is left.

We meet Bill at the kitchen table in the morning.

We listen carefully as he lays out his plans for escape.

He knows a guy from before the end of

the world who owns a yacht; keeps it secure in a harbor just up the coast.

He met him on the internet, but Bill knows where he lives. Some glass mansion up on the ridge.

It wouldn't be a stretch to drive up there with Mom's wagon. We could get his boat keys and then get the yacht and sail to some island.

Bill and his friend had discussed the plan before—Bill and his online group—in the context of a zombie apocalypse.

This wasn't that much different. They had nautical maps and had prepared. It wouldn't be hard.

Jan and I loaded the wagon with whatever food we could scavenge while Bill text messaged his friend (Paul) about initiating Operation Zombie Defense.

Paul gave the go ahead, and so we navigated the suburb streets and later, the empty highway, to meet him.

We run into trouble at the entrance to his neighborhood.

Merlin Estates is a series of cul-de-sacs off a crescent, nestled in the hills. It's surrounded by a twenty-foot iron fence that winds itself around the perimeter of the neighborhood.

The only entrance is a steel gate topped with spikes.

Before the apocalypse, it was showy—for the rich people that lived inside. It gave the place an air of Old World authenticity or something. Now though, it's an excellent defense, and the good people of Merlin Estates are using to their advantage too.

We're met by a platoon of black and silver SUVs parked before the closed gate, blocking the road perpendicular to the entrance. Assholes in polo shirts and golf pants with good, expensive haircuts and sunglasses smoke cigarettes and barbeque and drink champagne from a cooler set on the roadway. They clutch the finest semi-automatic sport shotguns their money has afforded them.

They stop us at the gate. Bill talks to them.

"Paul? Paul who?"

"I don't know his last name." Bill mutters. "I was in his online gaming group."

"His what?"

"Never mind."

"Take your shitty car and your teenagers back to the city."

Bill backs up the car, far enough down the road so that it's hidden from their view. He parks.

"Jeez." He mutters. "They organized quickly."

Jan squeezes me from the back seat and pecks me on the cheek. I happily note she still smells like shit.

"What do we do Bill?"

He bangs his palms on the steering wheel.

"Thinking. Thinking. Thinking. We need a distraction."

He eyes Jan.

"She's good looking."

I catch his drift.

"No way, Bill. That's not going to happen. Not even in your most depraved fantasies."

"What are we going to do? Go back to starve or get killed by the army? They'll be along eventually, you know. They won't have the Red Cross with them, either."

"There's no way I'm handing my girl over to you just so you can meet your dork pal and play commando. No fucking way."

Bill's eyes change. His face darkens. I instantly regret my wording and tone.

"This isn't a game, Alex." He whispers.

And that's when Bill attacks me with his knife.

This is the lowest part of my story.

There's a flash of steel and a flurry of movement as he produces the biggest buck knife I've ever seen from a leg sheath and tries to stab me in the heart. It happens so fast I barely have time to raise my hands to slow the attack.

There's a lot of screaming. Jan is trying to get him off of me. She's punching at his arms and shoulders. She's trying to knock the knife from his grasp and it isn't working.

But for all his military talk and his online friends and his apocalypse survival smarts, Bill isn't much of an athlete. In all his gun-tinkering and armchair commando escapades, he has never bothered to exercise or take any sort of proper training. If it got more difficult than reading some old military documents someone had posted to the newsgroup, or discussing the finer points of close-quarters chainsaw combat with Paul via instant message, Bill hasn't done it.

I could have held him off indefinitely, or at least until he got tired.

I could have.

I could have until he realizes he is outmatched against me.

He turns the knife on Jan.

He swivels in the driver's seat and slashes at her, catching her across the wrist, splattering blood across the roof of the car.

My protection instincts kick in and I grab his wrists and power his arms, the knife, backwards towards his body.

He kicks and thrashes, but he's got no leverage sitting down, and no clue what he's doing, really.

I power the knife forward and drive it into his chest, then lean hard on the handle and drive it right in.

It hits bone and stops at the midway point.

I jump a little.

The blade keeps going.

I get off when he stops moving. The knife is jammed into his breastbone, right to its blood-covered hilt.

Without dwelling on it, I open the door and kick him onto the road. Then I slide over and take the wheel.

I drive back home with Jan sobbing quietly beside me. She's shaking her head and pressing her injury into the car upholstery where it stains bright red—the same color as her lipstick.

She won't speak to me.

We eat the last can of cat food together later. I dig out an old candle from my parent's bedroom and light it. I put on an old Elton John record that we can listen to while we eat.

We don't talk.

We don't talk about the gas shortage or the riots or the looters that were coming to murder us in the night.

We don't talk about Bill, or Jan's hand, or Paul, or the ease in which I could lay on the knife as it punctured my struggling older brother's heart.

Instead, we eat and watch the candle and listen to the sound of piano as it drifts through the ruined house in silence.

I wonder what's going to happen to us.

We don't have sex afterwards.

In the morning, we break up.

I keep the dart gun and the wagon.

Meatloaf Of The Apocalypse

by
Deb Hoag

It all started with Milly Gifford's famous meatloaf. Or her mom's hip surgery, depending on how you looked at it. Most of the great catastrophes of Stanley Gifford's life could be traced back to Milly's mother in one way or another.

It was Tuesday, when she received the fateful phone call from her sister, Phoebe.

"Mill? It's mom. I mean, it's Phoebe, but I'm calling about mom. She's driving me crazy. I can't do anything right. I'm giving the plants too much water, and not putting enough salt in the oatmeal. The toast is too brown and the coffee's too light. If I don't get some help here, I'm going to kill her, and the whole hip surgery thing won't be a problem any more, because she'll have a butcher knife sticking out of one of her eyeballs. Except she'll probably tell me I should have used a carving knife, instead!"

By this point, Phoebe's voice had scaled the desperate heights of a middle-aged woman driven nearly to homicide by post-surgical nursing duties. And too much canasta.

Milly felt a twinge of guilt. So far, except for putting in an appearance at the hospital, bringing flowers and chocolate and a cute plush bear that said, "Get well beary soon!" embroidered across his stomach, Milly had done very little to contribute to her mother's successful recovery.

"Well," she began tentatively. "I could probably come down for a few days. I'd need to talk to Stan first, and wrap up some things here, but . . ."

Phoebe cut her off before she could get out another syllable.

"Thanks a mil, Mill! I'll tell Mom you'll be here tomorrow! Oh, my God, I appreciate this so much. Can you make it tomorrow by lunchtime? I'll start packing up my stuff so that you can get right into Mom's guest bedroom. Thanks, thanks, thanks! I'm going to tell Mom, now. She'll be so glad that you're finally going to come see her! Bye!"

Phoebe slammed the phone down before Milly could protest.

Milly sighed. Between Phoebe's desperation, gratitude and the small seasoning of guilt that she had tossed into the mix at the last minute, Milly hadn't stood a chance. She hoped Stan would understand.

II

Stan Gifford was the director of the Federal Department of Future Science Peacetime Research and Development. His interests had diversified since his early days at University of Michigan, when he had specialized in nuclear irradiation applications, but nuclear science was still his first love. Milly frequently remarked at cocktail parties that Stan had a remarkably even temper for someone who worked in such a volatile field, to which Stan inevitably replied, "and it's a good thing!" Their friends always laughed.

When Stan came home from work that night and found his wife packing for a lengthy stay with his mother-in-law, he accepted the news with surprising equanimity. His calm was due in part to the fact that he couldn't quite picture himself telling Milly what to do, regardless of the circumstances— her temperament eerily resembled her mother's, in some respects. Also contributing to his easy acquiescence was the fact that the only alternative he could see was to have Milly fetch her mother back to recuperate in Milly and Stan's home. And that would be a disaster of cataclysmic proportions.

In the face of his wife's imminent departure, Stan had only one request: "Milly, before you go, can you make me some of your meatloaf?"

"Stan, you Angel!" Milly patted Stan's shoulder amiably as she walked by. "Of course I can make you a meatloaf. I'll make a double-sized loaf and split it up into freezer containers so you can take it out and eat it whenever you want. I'm so glad you understand about Mother. She really needs her daughter right now." Milly was delighted that Stan would forgo the creature comforts afforded him by his state of matrimonial bliss in order to make sure his mother-in-law was well taken care of. She began pulling out the ingredients for her special meatloaf while they continued to chat about various odds and ends that would need to be handled by Stan while Milly was away.

One of the most interesting aspects of Stan's work, at least from Milly's point of view, was the experimental food preparation and modification projects that Stan supervised. Milly, who enthusiastically supported Stan's career—and the lavish salary which it produced—was a strong proponent of better living through nuclear irradiation.

The bread crumbs Milly used in her meatloaf were the product of a loaf of rye from which the ergot virus had been blasted with targeted nuclear particles. The water that moistened them was heavy. The tomatoes were genetically enhanced, the meat plumped with steroids and red dye #43.

The three eggs had been grown in a chemical bath that completely eliminated the need for actual chickens. The onions were nearly five years old, bacteria-free and perfectly preserved through the use of narrow spectrum bacterial agents, guaranteed to prevent decay and enzyme conversion for a minimum of . . . well, of a little over five years now.

On top, she sprinkled a nutritious cheese substitute created entirely from synthetics. The molecules were bound together with a sticky proton "glue" that one of Stan's junior researchers had come up with in his spare time.

While the meatloaf was bubbling merrily away in the microvection oven, Milly and Stan enjoyed garlic roasted chicken breast which had been harvested from vats instead of actual chickens. They dined by candlelight and toasted each other with a nice white wine made from blight and frost impervious grapes, the contribution of one of Stan's most prominent designer geneticists, Aubrey Winford. If there had been a Nobel Prize for the creation of the finest new white of the 21st Century, Aubrey would have won hands down.

After dinner, Milly sliced a commercially prepared triple-chocolate flavored torte, made entirely from artificial sweeteners and imitation chocolate. Even the fat that made the layers so lusciously moist was a fake—a celluloid-based derivative guaranteed to pass unabsorbed through the human digestive system. The wrapper proudly proclaimed "Irradiated Before Packaging - Refrigeration Not Needed!" and "The Amazing Diet Cake! The More You Eat, the More You Lose!" No one seemed to consider the potential for irony in that claim.

Stan measured out a scoop of freeze-dried coffee into each of their cups, heated water, and added hazelnut non-dairy creamer made from recycled motor oils through the use of split-neutron reconfiguration therapy. Milly pulled the meatloaf out of the oven and set it in the macrowave to extract the excess heat energy.

By the time Milly had licked the last of the whipped chocolate-flavored artificial topping off her fork, Stan was sighing contentedly and patting his stomach. The meatloaf was cool enough to slice and pack into plastic containers and store in the freezer, which ran silently on an atomic power pack that would not need to be recharged for several lifetimes. Stan actually teared up at the thought of doing without Milly for several weeks. But the thought was immediately quelled when he considered the alternative—his mother-in-law Freida, up front and personal, sitting in his favorite chair, clutching his remote greedily with her crimson coated talons, barking out orders and opinions with no appreciation whatsoever for the man who pays the satellite bill. The picture made him shudder, and immediately quelled his sentimentality.

So Stan stood up and stacked the dinner dishes in the waterless UV cleaning cabinet. When he was done, he turned to Milly and gave her a loving smile. "Honey," he said, "let me help you pack."

Sailing along on the smooth sea of protracted matrimonial complacency, Stan and Milly retired for the night.

II

For the first two nights, things went well for Stan, and between his well-organized domesticity and Milly's numerous phone calls, it hardly felt as if she were gone. As the weekend approached, Stan felt a certain amount of ambivalence about having two whole days without anyone to admire him, or to give him the deferential treatment he knew he so richly deserved. Milly wasn't one of his research assistants, but she did fill up the weekend void quite nicely.

Pondering this, Stan called up one of his old college buddies, and they agreed to meet on Friday after work for drinks and a few laughs.

Two seconds after Stan sat down at the table with Todd Wisner, he realized that the idea had been a terrible error. They hadn't even got their first beers when Todd started telling Stan about his recent divorce. By the time the second round arrived, Stan knew more about Todd than he had ever dreamed—or nightmared. Stan did his best to zone completely out and not register a single sordid detail.

"I was in bad shape after the divorce," Todd said.

Stan didn't really think Todd was in any better shape now, but refrained from stating the obvious.

"Then I met Sylvia, and she helped me see that I was having a massive spiritual backlash from all the globally toxic work I had done. She told me that the only way to clean up my karmic record in this lifetime would be to immerse myself in Naderism and achieve a complete ethical and moral rebirth."

Todd shifted in his seat, and leaned forward to look earnestly into Stan's face. "And she was right! I can't tell you how much better I feel now. I'm a twenty-first century spiritual ecology convert. I'm alive, Stan! More alive than I've felt in years! Last week, I protested at an assembly of the National Nuclear Advisory Board. It was great! I almost got hit with a baton. And, they were going to arrest me for disturbing the peace, but I wasn't loud enough."

Todd looked apologetic. "I had a little bit of a cold that day. Just couldn't get up to full volume. Maybe next time."

Stan could see where this was going. Next, Todd would be trying to turn him into a Naderite. Renounce his job, ride a bicycle, and get into confrontations with the police. That'd be the day!

Todd showed no signs of slowing up. He covered the energy crisis, global warming and animal extinction in the time it took for Stan to toss back a shot of Jim Beam. When he started in on nuclear waste, genetic modification and chaos mutation theory, Stan swallowed another shot of whiskey and made his excuses.

On the cab ride home, an inebriated Stan thought darkly about Todd's sudden change of attitude on nuclear science. Todd hadn't complained when his nuclear research salary was paying for his house, college for his two kids, and silicon-gel bust enhancement surgery for his first wife. Smug bastard! Without nuclear experimentation, he wouldn't have anything to protest about. Even being officially out of the field, it was still the center of his life.

Fueled with soggy indignation, Stan paid the cab driver, and decided to console himself with some of Milly's meatloaf. And maybe another shot of whiskey.

By the time Stan made it into the kitchen, he was feeling sorry for himself on multiple levels. Milly had deserted him. Even with a satellite dish capable of pulling in over five thousand channels, there was nothing on TV even remotely interesting. And Todd was on his way to his new condo, to sleep with a girl young enough to be Stan's daughter.

He pulled out a package of frozen meatloaf, and put it in the microvecter. Then he had another shot of whiskey while he waited for his food to heat.

Finally, the little electronic chime sounded, and Stan pulled out the meatloaf. Grabbing a glass of soy milk, Stan flung himself sulkily into his recliner, mentally taunting his mother-in-law with her inability to oust him from his favorite chair.

The first bite was a balm to his troubled soul, tangy and hearty and filling that ancient need for comfort food that has existed since Eve went out shopping and left Adam at home to keep an eye on Cain and Abel.

The second bite was ambrosia—a flood of culinary delight on his tongue that assured him that everything in Stan's world was just as it should be.

The third bite, though . . . was still semi-frozen. Stan blinked at his dinner in amazement, then spat the cold meatloaf back onto the plate. He tentatively nudged the middle of the remaining meatloaf with this fork. Was that an ice crystal? Stan's eyes narrowed as they traveled from his food to the microvecter, in plain sight across the hall on a kitchen counter.

Offended into a semblance of sobriety, Stan set his meatloaf down and grabbed a screwdriver. He wasn't the Director of the Federal Department of Future Science Peacetime Research and Development for nothing, By God! The microvection industry was about to be treated to a hands-on consultation by Stan Gifford, PhD.

Two hours later, he admitted defeat.

Stan had begun the project with enthusiasm, feeling much better about the whole wretched weekend, now that he had a purpose. He tore down and examined all the microvection unit components, assemblies and chained microchip command units. He made colorful schematics and took digital photographs of everything inside the housing from start to finish. And he couldn't come up with a single change that would improve the functionality or the wave distribution of the damnable thing!

At midnight, he called Mike Smith. His lead R & D man blinked sleepily into the camera phone. "Hey, Boss! What's up?"

"Emergency project, Mike. Take a look at these schematics for me, would you? I need a couple of suggestions for how to goose up the power and the radiation spread."

Mike's eyes sharpened with interest. "Power source?"

Stan held up a palm-sized fusion generator, which he had been carrying around for a couple of weeks, looking for ways to justify the money that had been appropriated for its creation.

"Sweet! When do you need this by?"

If Stan was going to enjoy a hot dinner on Saturday, it would have to be fast. "Four this afternoon. Can you do it?"

"Rush job, huh? First Strike Department, I bet. Those boys always need everything yesterday. I was supposed to go antiquing with Tina tomorrow afternoon, but what the hell. National Security takes precedence over junk buying any day. Right?"

Stan and Mike exchanged the superior looks of married men who have just managed to out-think a wife, and Stan hit the transmit button that would send all his data to Mike's unit. Mike seemed so happy to escape Tina's weekend mission that Stan didn't have the heart to tell him it wasn't National Security at all, just a lonely man on a quest for a hot dinner. Surely that was important, too? As important as any demand made by the First Strike Department—there hadn't been a war in years! Well, there had been the Buda vs. Pest skirmish. And the Lichtenstein Revolt. And the Basque-Algeria conflict. But war? Not for years!

Stan went to sleep content in the knowledge that by this time tomorrow, all his problems would be solved.

II

The next morning, Stan woke up bright-eyed and raring to go. He had cold cereal with artificial marshmallow bits and soy milk, while sitting on his patio and contemplating a dinner-time meatloaf binge of epic proportions. With the engineering problem in Mike's capable hands, Stan was sure the solution was imminent. Sure enough, his faithful R & D man called him at two o'clock —a full two hours before the deadline Stan had imposed.

Mike's face was gaunt and gray, his eyes were bloodshot, but his grin was triumphant. "Boss? I found the solution. Massive power boost, broad wave dispersion, and absolutely silent—no one will ever hear it coming! Do they need it on wheels?"

Stan started to ask him what the hell he was talking about, and remembered just in time that Mike thought this was some kind of First Strike Department weapon.

"No, no, Mike. They already have a transport and delivery system ready to go. Just needed a good brain from our department to make sure it works once they get it there!"

"Work? It's gonna knock their socks off! Want me to send you back the revised schematics?"

"Do that, Mike! And then tell Tina to treat you nice and let you take a nap—I'll make sure your Holiday-Formerly-Known-As-Christmas bonus is a good one this year!"

"Anything that lets her do more shopping! Thanks, Boss! Let me know how it works." Mike's yawn was so big that Stan could hear his jaw pop. As soon as the schematics started streaming across the screen, Stan hit print and cut the connection.

Hmm. That Mike was a clever guy. Stan thought maybe he would keep the promise he made about Mike's bonus this year.

Gathering the printouts, Stan headed downstairs to start upgrading his microvecter.

II

By six o'clock, the Stan was screwing the housing back together over the reconfigured circuits. The atomic battery was riding high on a rivet-mounted box on the back of the plate, a job Stan was rather proud of. Mike had managed to make marvelous use of the souped up power source, and Stan was quite excited about the test run. Maybe this would be the breakthrough idea he had been looking for—something that would allow him to take an early retirement and end his enslavement to scientific bureaucracy forever. Of course, he would have to wait to patent and hawk it in the public sector, and probably have to cut Mike in—if Mike ever realized what he had done. Not likely—his R & D guy would be looking for his work to show up in something that went "boom!", not in a handy household appliance.

With that last beatific thought, Stan put the meatloaf in the microvecter—no, the Stanovecter!—set the time and hit the start button with his thumb.

Barely a second later, the phone rang. He would have ignored it, but it was Milly's ring, and if he didn't pick up, she'd just call over and over until he did. Forcing a smile on his face, he walked out onto the patio and answered the phone as he sank into one of the comfy, cushioned seats of their waterproof-imitation rattan furniture.

Milly's face flickered into life on the screen. "Hi, Sweetie! I miss you so much!"

"I miss you too, Dear. I was just heating up some of your special meatloaf and thinking about the angel who cooked it for me."

Milly fluttered her lashes. "What a sweet thing to say. Oh, Stan! I have some good news! You'll never guess."

Stan sighed. "If I'll never guess, why don't you just tell me, Milly?"

Milly gave him a steely look.

He pasted an interested look on his face. "Mother is doing better?"

Instantly, Milly's good humor was restored. She actually clapped her hands together. "That's it! Exactly right, Stan. Mom went to the doctor today, and he said that she's ready to start rehab. Another week, and she'll be right as rain, and I'll be coming home . . . Darling?"

Alerted by the change in her tone, Stan forced himself to focus on his wife again. "What, Milly?"

She cocked her head to one side. "Stan, what's that green glow? Behind you. It looks like it's coming from . . . my *kitchen*?"

Stan whipped his head around, and gazed open mouthed as a luminous green foam exploded out of the Stanovecter and effervesced over the counters, up the walls and down onto the floor.

Stan could hear Milly wailing over his shoulder, but it was hard to take his eyes off the gelatinous green ooze. It was mind boggling. It was incredible. It was . . . Milly's Meatloaf, come to an ungodly, terrifying life.

Even as he realized the meatloaf was moving on its own, , there was a reluctant, squelching sound, and an eyelid formed and popped open, revealing a monstrous eye that whirled wildly in its socket until it spotted Stan. The mass began to ooze purposefully toward him, and it was only the adrenaline born of pure terror that gave him the strength to leap off the patio and over the low hedge that edged their backyard.

Rushing to a neighbor's house, Stan pounded on the door until Milton pulled it open crankily. "Milt! It's an emergency, I need to use your phone right now!"

Milt gave him a sour look. "You forgettin' to pay the phone bill does not constitute an emergency situation on my part." But he held the door wide and waved Stan in.

Stan knew the number to the OSHA Department of Experiments Gone Wrong Emergency Clean-Up Division by heart—they all did, it was drilled into them at work the same way they were drilled on fire exits and Experimental Subjects' Radiation Break Schedules.

Within two minutes, the WECUP truck was screeching to a halt in front of Milt's house, where several dozen neighbors had joined Stan in contemplating the green glob that now engulfed his entire brown brick pseudo-Tudor ranch home. As he watched, the last of his patio furniture disappeared down the ravenous maw. The WECUP responders wasted no time.

"You Stanley Gifford?"

"Yes."

"Federal Department of Future Science Peacetime Research and Development?"

"Yes."

"Kitchen experiment gone wrong?"

"Yes."

Can you tell us what appliance you were attempting to modify, Sir?"

"Microvecter." Stan hung his head in shame.

"And the food item the modified microvecter interacted with?"

"Meatloaf."

With a surprising touch of humanity, the WECUP agent laid a comforting hand on Stan's shoulder.

"Wife out of town?"

Stan nodded miserably.

"It's hard to resist the vision of a nice hot meatloaf, Sir. I can't condone it, but we've seen worse."

Stan looked up, hope dawning in his eyes, but the sympathetic WECUP Agent had already turned away to confer with one of his colleagues.

"It's a 207 situation, Bob."

"Is that the meatloaf, or the pot roast?"

"Meatloaf, big guy. You know what that means."

The other agent nodded his head solemnly. "Time to bring out the atomic cockroaches?"

"Atomic cockroaches?" said Stan.

The friendly agent nodded. "Mutated. They really saved our cookies in the Great Irradiated Jello Salad Incident of '34. They'll eat anything. After it's all over, we pick up 'em back up with vacuum hoses that have a built in geiger-counter. Nice thing about the radiation trail. We can always track 'em back down. Only thing on the planet that can stop a modified microvecter meatloaf once it's on the move."

Stan watched as they pointed the cockroach cage at the meatloaf and prepared to open the door. He made a mental note to take Mike off the Holiday-that-used-to-be-Christmas list.

The Art Of Survival

by Steven Archer

The older I get the more I realize the old saying "time is money" is backwards. Money, it turns out, is time.

When it comes right down to it, of all the choices in life - the one at the core, the one that most drastically effects your life is what you will do with your time here on this planet. What are your priorities? What are you driven to do? What are you bringing to humanities table, as it were. What is your carrot? When you go to bed at night, and you look at your contribution to the world, what is your justification for the last 24 hours of your life? How have you made your life, and perhaps the lives of others, a more interesting place?

It's an important question, and naturally the answer is different for everyone. I have several friends whose goals in life are to be comfortable, travel, watch television, etc. They are satisfied trading eight hours out of twenty four for the money that allows them to live the way they want to live. For others the most satisfying thing in their life is their children. For some it's accumulating wealth for the sake of keeping score. All acceptable goals, as long as they are happy with their choices.

That is not my path nor, I suspect, if you are reading this, is it yours. For me, satisfaction comes from making things and putting them out into the world. I think I can honestly say that at no time in my life have I seen myself with a nine to five job - not happily anyway. Not because I am lazy or unwilling to work. As anyone with a career in the arts can tell you, if you choose this life, the only time you are not working is when you are asleep and even then, there is probably something you *should* be doing.

My earliest memories are of making things, drawing with crayon on construction paper, gluing assorted pastas to dinnerware, and so on. I have spent years in school honing those skills, and many more, scraping up money for food in order to paint, write music, and generally continue my career.

Before I get into this next bit, I should get the whole "selling out" thing out of the way. For me "selling out" is creating work that goes against your beliefs, or that you would not be inclined to make for any reason other than to sell it. Creating work that means something to you that you also hope to sell is, at least from where I sit, not selling out. I recognize that for some, the idea of selling any work somehow compromises their artistic principals. Fortunately, these tend to be the same people who believe that starving and being broke somehow equals credibility. So that works out well for them. In my experience, it is hard to create anything on an empty stomach.

If you choose to live the life of a full time artist, it becomes essential that you learn to create work that is likely to sell.

For now, let us put the technical part aside, and assume you have the ability to produce work of unsurpassed quality. Now, that we have established that, the next trick is learning to think of yourself as a business

The first part of this is embracing the fact that creation is your career. Believe in the intrinsic value of your work, and the time you put into it. If you don't see the value in it, no one else will.

Second, no one is going to come by your studio and discover you. You have to go to your audience. Get your work out there in whatever way you can, go online, get art shows, sit down in a public place and show it to passers by (till the cops show up and make you move), do whatever it takes to learn who your market is. Who does your work appeal to?

Third, once you identify your market and your vector for sales, you must find your price point. That is, the balance between the amount of time you put into a piece vs the likely price it will sell at. For example, it's all well and good to spend 6 months painting a beautiful five foot by five foot piece with a price tag of $5000, however for most part, unless you are very well known, you probably won't (at least not often) see a return on your time investment. Conversely you can bring the size, and the amount of time invested into any given piece, down and sell them for less. Which makes them affordable to a larger number of people, increasing your sales potential.

Fourth, learn to sell yourself. Learn to talk about the work, the why of it, the what of it. Listen to questions, have clear answers, learn to love the people that find the work interesting. Learn to be a conduit for the ideas behind the art.

You are it's spokesperson.

Fifth, Never take your audience for granted, they are not there for your benefit. Treating them as such puts a bullet in your career.

While it is sometimes necessary to change yourself, you are not obliged to change your creative vision to suit the masses. Quite the contrary, go out and find people who see things a similar way, tap them on the shoulder and say to them, "This is how I see things, and I would very much like to show it to you."

Ahlana Demona

by

MP Johnson

I.

Peter slouched in his chair, the only one in the audience not laughing. On stage, James Smiley performed the famous undead stilt act of his popular magic show, "Abra Cadaver." With each of his feet strapped to the head of a trained corpse, he paraded high above the ground. As the zombies carried the magician around, he held his arms outstretched, looking magnificent as undead doves fluttered out from the sleeves of his turquoise suit.

Peter didn't see anything magnificent about it. He saw the event as pure exploitation or, as he liked to call it, deadsploitation. The way the magician treated his costars was nothing short of a violation of every human's rights—alive or dead. In fact, he had made it his mission to stop as many people as possible from supporting the show.

Tonight, he had failed miserably.

Minutes earlier, he had been leading his zombie rights group—DDL, short for Dead Deserve Life—in a protest. As usual, he had been confronting patrons with facts about the undead, exposing the pain and humiliation the corpses suffered as part of the show. He had put himself in the face of one girl who, through a combination of charm and brute force, got him to enter the very event he had been trying to shut down.

Now this girl sat next to him, her thick purple lips turned up in a big smile. Watching her chuckle at the way Smiley pretended to lose balance and almost fall off his corpse chariots made Peter feel ashamed to be there. He had abandoned his cause. The group outside would certainly notice his absence.

He got up to leave.

"No. It's just getting good," the woman said, grabbing his shoulder and shoving him back into his seat.

He didn't resist. Even though he knew this would lead to nothing good, he couldn't help staring at her. She had beautiful lime-green eyes, and the brows above them were perfect black streaks. He followed her sharp cheekbones to her ears and the huge silver hoops that dangled from them. A high ponytail held her thick black hair in place.

Peter turned his head to the stage to watch the grand finale. The magician ushered an emaciated male zombie onto the stage. Dressed in a tuxedo, the corpse gazed at the crowd with a lipless grin on his face.

Smiley pulled a bone saw from behind his back and cut through the dead man's forehead. The zombie kept smiling as the bit of blood that hadn't dried up in his veins trickled between his eyes and dripped off the mangled tip of his nose.

Finished sawing, Smiley wiped the sweat off his brow with a purple handkerchief. With great care, he removed the sawed-off skull cap. He reached into the head slowly. A surprised look took over his face as he pulled out a little brown bunny.

The corpse dropped to the floor.

"I guess what they say is true," the magician said. "Life really does come out of death."

The crowd went crazy as colored stage lights flashed and Smiley vanished into a cloud of smoke.

The woman stood and squeezed past Peter, who couldn't help but stare at the perfect bottom hidden beneath her tight skirt. She seized his hand and pulled him toward the stage. Peter didn't fight as the woman shoved through the retreating crowd and into a door labeled "Employees only," eventually bursting into the magician's dressing room.

"Ms. Ahlana Demona, the infamous monster hunter. What a pleasure," Smiley said.

"I wish I could say the same," she purred. "Let's get straight to business. Zombies are killing people. Zombies don't usually kill people. You know zombies. So what do you know about zombies killing people?"

"Why don't you ask your friend, Mr. DDL here? The show didn't sell out tonight because of the antics of him and his group of dead-lovers. Surely he knows zombies better than me."

Ahlana turned to Peter.

"I've heard whisperings throughout the undead community," he responded, surprised at how ridiculous the lie sounded when he said it out loud.

In reality, his knowledge of the matter didn't extend beyond that presented to him by the evening news. Almost daily reports of people being murdered and partially eaten had led many to speculate that zombies were responsible. Peter didn't believe it. The dead were extremely docile. After the first rising, they had committed a slew of murders. Further investigation indicated the majority were self-defense. Corpses were just trying to survive in the face of confrontation by overzealous, self-styled zombie hunters. After a few weeks, everything settled down and, except for a few random murders committed by zombies—which were greatly outnumbered by those committed by living people—everyone realized the dead weren't the mindless killing machines they had been made out to be.

"What do you mean by whisperings?" Ahlana asked, lowering her thin brows just the right way to make it clear she saw through Peter's bullshit.

"If I heard anything important, I would have gone to the police," he said, deciding not to take his bluff any further. "It's crucial to catch the bad ones. These crimes are adding to negative feelings toward a group of people that are, for the most part, harmless to a fault."

Ahlana rolled her eyes. "Your turn, Smiley."

"What makes you think I have anything to do with this?"

"Oh, cut the innocent act."

"Yeah, you're a murderer!" Peter chimed in.

A scowl fell over the magician's face, directly contradicting his last name. "Murderer? These people are dead. D-E-A-D. They're just hollow shells walking around. This is no second life. The only crime happening at my shows is the harassment of innocent patrons out for a night of entertainment by you and your corpse-loving militia."

"Bullshit! These are good people with lingering memories and emotions. They have rights and you're slaughtering them for cheap laughs."

Smiley moved closer to Peter, clenching his fists.

"Hey, I'm the boss here," Ahlana shouted. She pointed at Peter, "You shut up with your liberal nonsense," then looked at Smiley, "and you explain what the hell is going on."

The magician quickly regained his composure and stepped back, which relieved Peter. "Do you believe in werewolves, Ms. Demona?"

"I believe in werewolves. I believe in slime-sucking closet beasts, nuns possessed by giant brain leeches and many other things, but werewolves haven't murdered a human in years. Why would they start now?"

"What better time? Who's getting blamed?" Smiley replied.

"Gotcha." Ahlana said.

"Now, if you wouldn't mind finding your own way out, I need to prepare for the late show."

Peter followed Ahlana to the exit. Outside, he was disappointed and relieved to see that his group had gone home. Disappointed that the mismatched crew of activists and college students didn't have the stamina to stay and protest the evening's second performance. Relieved that he would have plenty of time to think of a good explanation for his disappearance.

As he walked toward his car, the woman shouted after him.

"I'm going to find a werewolf. You want to come with?"

He paused and turned around, careful not to fall into the habit of blurting "yes" to anything a pretty girl asked him. "Why would I want to do that?" he asked, the resistance in his voice coming out like a soggy lump of clay.

"Well, you answered that your-self earlier, didn't you? It's important to catch whoever is responsible for this, cause it's giving zombies a bad name. This is what a real activist would do."

Peter couldn't help but smile. "Good answer."

He followed her to a black cargo van taking up two parking spots in the lot across the street.

Peter climbed in and watched Ahlana as she jumped into the driver's seat. "It isn't even cold out. Why are you wearing that sweatshirt?" he asked, immediately regretting the new addition to his collection of weird questions and comments he had made to attractive girls at awkward times.

"Check this out," she said, grabbing the zipper between her fingertips, which were accented by long purple nails, and pulling. Strapped to the inside of the sweatshirt was an array of knives, stakes and even throwing stars, which he had never seen in real life.

He caught his gaze slipping from the weapons to the push-up bra cleavage peeking out of her red tank top. Looking up, he met her eyes. She had caught him staring.

"You're an easy one to reel in, aren't you?" she asked, raising her eyebrows. "Here comes the hard part," she whispered to herself before saying to Peter, "I guess that stare is my cue to provide an important disclosure: I'm not exactly what you expect in a girl," she said.

"What?"

"Well, I've got stuff other chicks don't have. I'm what the textbooks call a pre-operative male-to-female transsexual."

"A shemale?"

Through gritted teeth, she replied, "If you ever call me that again I'll kick your fucking ass."

"Why? What's wrong with that?" Peter asked, feeling as if he was trailing behind the conversation and somehow scrambling to catch up.

"The same thing that's wrong with calling a Chinese person a chink, or a black person a nigger, or referring to your undead friends as fertilizer bags."

"I see." He turned away for a moment to look at the setting sun and wait for all the feelings of attraction toward her to drain out of his body. They didn't. He reminded himself that he wasn't into men, no matter how beautiful they appeared to be. The confused part of him wanted to hop out of the van and run. Luckily, that part was outvoted by the intelligent, open-minded part; the part that remembered that his whole mission in life was to get equal treatment for people who hadn't been getting it.

He reached out to shake. "My name's Peter Timbaro."

"I'm Ahlana Demona. Nice to meet you," she replied, taking his hand.

As they drove through the Milwaukee streets, Peter turned in his seat and looked into the back of the van. Other than the blood-stained scrap of carpet, the only decorations were a series of chains and cuffs bolted to the sides. Realizing what they were for, he asked, "What prompts a person to want to murder monsters?"

Without taking her eyes of the road, she answered flatly, "Revenge."

After a lengthy pause, she elaborated. "I lived in New Orleans for awhile, where I met a guy at one of those cheesy voodoo shops in the French Quarter. I guess you could call him my first love. He wasn't the type of guy you would expect to work there, not nerdy or fragile or goth. This guy was big and buff." She emphasized the statement by taking her hand off the wheel and flexing her bicep.

"That didn't really matter, of course. I certainly don't mind nerds," she said, turning to wink at Peter.

He grinned. Part of him wanted to say that he wasn't attracted to her, just in case she had the wrong idea. He couldn't tell if her wink was serious or if she was just being silly. Hell, he didn't even know if a wink could be serious. Also, part of him still wasn't sure that he wasn't attracted to her.

"I'll admit that the muscles were nice," she continued, "but what was most important was that he accepted me."

Ahlana's long lashes fluttered as her eyelids tried to cut off tears. Peter wondered if he should interrupt her and steer the conversation toward a more positive topic. The first one that popped into his mind was zombie rights. He decided just to let her keep talking.

"I told him the truth about me and he told me the truth about him. I was a transsexual, he was a monster hunter. Every night, he would sneak out to slay vampires and goat-suckers. Every night, I would harass him to take me along. Eventually, he started showing me some martial arts moves. One night, he decided I was ready. We went out to the swamp to kill this muck monster that folks out there had been complaining about.

"When we found it, we realized neither of us was ready. It trudged out of the weeds, opened its mouth and unleashed this blast of tentacles. They knocked me out of the way. I crawled over to my guy. His face had been crushed. He wasn't moving."

She paused again, her lips taught as she held in the emotion.

"What did you do?" Peter asked.

"I did the only thing I could do. I ran. I ran all the way back to Wisconsin."

Peter didn't know what to say.

"Then, when I learned that Wisconsin had monsters too, I started training and went into business," she added, trying to sound upbeat.

"Why did you go to New Orleans in the first place?"

"Wow. You're just Mr. Twenty Questions, aren't you? Let me guess. You picked up an issue of some chick mag and read an article that told you how women like to think men are interested in them? Right?"

He gazed out the window. "I'm sorry for prying."

"No. It's cool," she said, smiling amiably. "It was the winters. Wisconsin winters suck."

Peter could agree with that. "They can get a little messy."

"Especially when you're fifteen and homeless because you have parents that are too closed-minded to accept that their son is actually their daughter."

"That must have been hard," Peter said, realizing how bad he was at listening to emotional stories. He could never come up with the right things to say. Realizing how selfish the thought was, he chided himself. After all, listening to them wasn't nearly as hard as living them.

"It can't even be put into words. Luckily, I found other girls like me in New

Orleans. I found out how to get hormones. When I was old enough, I even got a job at a strip joint that specialized in girls like me. That's where I got my name. Man, the things you can learn from a transsexual stripper."

Ahlana grinned slyly. "Okay. My turn. What do you do?"

"I just finished college," Peter said, glad to have the focus switch to his much more boring life, which he happened to love to talk about. "Since then, I've been working to become a Certified Independent Social Worker specializing in families that have had dead relatives come back into their lives. There's a serious gap that leaves families with no one to help them deal with the unique stresses that come when a deceased loved one returns. I'd like to be the first to fill that gap."

"The world needs more good social workers. Do you have a girlfriend?"

"Yes," he said. The question took him by surprise. He paused and wondered if he should correct himself, feeling his face turning red under the pressure. "Actually, no," he blurted out. "She left me after school."

"That's a bummer. Let me guess. She wasn't into zombie activism?"

"Not really. She wanted to get out of Milwaukee and go to Los Angeles. I told her I had made too much progress with DDL to abandon it."

He hesitated for a moment before adding, "She said I only loved dead people. 'Why don't you just screw them, too?' That's the last thing she said to me."

Peter decided to change the subject, realizing this conversation had already gotten way too personal. "What made you pull me inside the show with you anyway?"

"You were so serious, listing off reasons why I shouldn't go in. I thought it would be funny," she said, grinning.

"You've got a weird sense of humor."

"I know. Okay, so, even though I originally did it for my own amusement, I realized you would be helpful, what with your zombie expertise and all. I could use an assistant."

"I don't think I'm cut out for it, really."

"It's okay. You can be the brains. I'll be the brawn."

They pulled into the parking lot an empty apartment complex on the edge of the city.

Ahlana pointed a long nail at the night sky. "Check it out."

Peter looked up at the full moon, its yellow light shining down hard enough to illuminate the blacktopped lot.

"I used to live on the third floor, but the owner cleared the place out," she explained. "He thought he was going to make a good chunk of change turning it into an undead assisted living facility. It didn't take."

"Why not?"

"Beats me. Maybe nobody wanted to pay for corpse daycare."

This information hit Peter hard. His whole future was based on the assumption that people cared just as deeply about their dead relatives as they did their living ones. He had seen plenty of families take in their deceased with open arms and he was ready to do the same. Fortunately, his parents were still alive and well—as were both sets of grandparents—but when that status changed, he would be there for them.

A clicking sound drew his attention to a second floor window. Inside, a corpse poked at the glass. From the looks of it, the dead man had spent some time repeating the motion. His finger bent upwards at the middle knuckle. Bone protruded through the thin flesh, tapping against the window. "Looks like they have one taker."

"Undead squatters."

"Well, what are we doing here?" Peter asked.

"I'm meeting an ex-boyfriend."

"Ooookay."

"Actually, he's a werewolf," she said, speaking in a lowered voice, as if doing so could obscure the obvious problem with such a statement.

"You dated a werewolf?" Peter asked, incredulous.

"I seriously intended to kill him," she said apologetically, "but he was covered with cool tattoos. All these flaming eyeballs and robot claws. I totally crushed out on him. One thing led to the next, but the relationship didn't last."

"Because he found out you killed people like him?"

"Actually, he didn't mind the monster hunter angle as much as he did the whole trans thing. God! If only guys could love without getting all analytical about it and questioning their sexuality. Who the fuck cares? Turns out it was for the best. He's kind of a go-nowhere type. You know, the kind that spends all day on the couch playing videogames with no intention of motivating? I'm totally going to mess with him. You stay out of sight"

Peter followed her orders. Hiding behind a corner, he watched as she made her way across a sea of blacktop to a row of garages that sat opposite the apartment building. The tips of her shoes clanged against green metal as she hoisted herself onto a dumpster, then climbed onto the roof of the parking complex.

He stared at Ahlana, framed by the full moon as she waited for her prey. She pulled her long hair out of the ponytail, letting it blow gently in the breeze. The locks were so thick and black they looked like a hole had been punched in the night, sucking in all excess light. His biggest difficulty was not believing that her gorgeous, pale legs, with their calves pushed up to perfect curves by her high-heeled shoes, could possibly belong to someone who spent her life hunting monsters. The hardest thing to comprehend was that between those smooth legs were male parts.

A few minutes later, Peter smiled and watched as a scrawny wolfman crept across the lot, keeping close to the shadows of the garage. Its fur, gray with specks of brown, hadn't been kept tidy. The matted shag formed dreadlocks that rattled against each other as he moved. After catching himself wondering why a girl like Ahlana would even spend a week with a thing like that, he reminded himself that he didn't care. Her business was her business.

When Ahlana's target was under her, she dove off the roof. She wrapped a chain around the beast's neck and pressed her knee against its spine. As she shouted questions into its ear, the wolf dug his claws under the chain, struggling for air. The monster's responses were choked snarls, barely audible where Peter stood.

Finished with the interrogation, Ahlana let the chain loose. The wolf whimpered and ran off.

Peter came out of hiding and walked across the parking lot toward Ahlana. He couldn't help but think how beautiful she was, regardless of what was between her legs. At the same time, he felt ashamed for thinking it. Then he felt ashamed for feeling ashamed. Then he just felt pissed off for being one of those guys who got all analytical about attraction.

"According to my unbathed friend Dwight, there is a werewolf think tank behind the murders. Guess who's in charge?"

"A werewolf?"

"Exactly. But, oddly enough, a werewolf named James Smiley."

"Whoa."

"That bitch is the werewolf mastermind."

"What does a werewolf think tank do?" Peter asked as Ahlana's heels clicked on the blacktop, making their way toward the van.

"According to Dwight, the werewolves have taken an interest in the arts. Their goal is to create brilliant paintings, music, films and so on. When they have gotten appropriate recognition and are considered the foremost artists of the 21st century, they plan to reveal themselves as werewolves, ideally creating vast acceptance for their kind, then merging back into mainstream society, not unlike what you want to help zombies do now. The think tank was formed to create the most efficient and logical path toward that goal."

"What does such a bizarre and meandering plan have to do with murder?"

"I don't know, but I'm damn sure going to get Smiley to tell us," she said. "But first, I want leather on for this . . . and something pink."

∏

Ahlana introduced Peter to her apartment. "Here's the tour: This is the living room," she spread her arms toward the red carpeted area covered with a jumble of mismatched furniture.

"And my bedroom is over there. Don't look. It's totally messy. The bathroom is through that door. Check out my spare bedroom—or, as I like to call it, my armory—while I get changed."

Peter shrugged his shoulders and went into the other room. One wall was covered with sports equipment hanging from racks, everything from chipped croquet mallets to bent golf clubs. He looked over the series of baseball bats—some metal, but mostly wood—of varying sizes, covered with dried blood. In addition, one corner contained a pile of stakes carved from old chair legs and tree branches.

He could barely walk without tripping on something, be it a pair of fingerless gloves or a couple of power drills.

"Hey! What do you do with these drills?" He picked one up and guessed the answer as dried blood flaked off the bit.

"You're going to hate me for this, but when the zombies rose, I took a pro-active approach and killed a shitload of them. I found that just walking up to them and drilling a hole in their forehead was more efficient than trying to stick them with knives or smash their skulls with a baseball bat," she yelled from the other room. "Do you know how many pounds of pressure it takes to smash a human skull?"

"No."

"Neither do I, but it's enough to totally mess up my manicure."

"Why don't you just use a gun?"

"Oh please. Guns are for sissies."

This comment made Peter snicker.

Ahlana emerged from her bedroom clad in a pink sweatshirt and a leather skirt that went down to her knees. On the hood of her sweatshirt, the word "bitch" was written in old English letters. She wore extremely high heels. Coldly, she stared at him, her hands on her hips. "What's so funny?"

"Nothing. Obviously, you're no sissy. What are you going to do if you need to run?" He asked, pointing at her heels.

"I won't need to run."

"Ahhhh."

"I'm just going to fix my makeup and then we can go."

"Why do you need makeup? To impress Smiley, or his zombie friends?"

She appeared again with the same hands-on-hips stance. "For your information, women don't necessarily wear makeup for men. Not everything is done to cater to you guys. Sometimes we just like to look hot for ourselves. It makes us feel good."

"Is that even more important for you?" Peter put down the drill and looked Ahlana in her eyes, making sure she was clear that he was serious and not trying to imply anything negative. He wasn't sure where things were going, obviously nowhere romantic, but he didn't want to rule out a possible friendship with any stupid questions.

"It used to be. I haven't had trouble feeling like a woman for quite a few years."

For a second, Peter thought about complementing her on how feminine she was, but held back. He didn't want her to get the wrong idea.

"Are you ever going to have your thing removed?"

"Wow. Going into the hardcore stuff, huh? I don't know. A lot of girls like me just jump into it like it's no big deal, which blows my mind. I'm kind of a wuss with surgery. I could barely handle the pain of my implants and my nose job. Also, there's a part of me that think it's selling out. I would just be conforming to society's definition of what a woman should be. I'm not into conforming. I'm into redefining."

Peter followed her to the bathroom and watched her coat her thick lips with pink gloss. Finished, she stared at herself in the mirror for a moment, first head on, then sideways.

"I'm ready to go."

Π

They parked outside the back door of the theater. Soon, Smiley emerged and got into his brand-new SUV, driving off with a young female in tow. Despite her sexy clothes, the girl was obviously dead. Blood glistened in the moonlight as it streamed out of a crack in the side of her skull.

They followed at a distance, stopping eventually at a plain brick building downtown. They waited in the van until the magician and his corpse lady disappeared through a green metal door.

"Hey, what are we going to do? Kill him?" Peter asked.

"Let's play it by ear," Ahlana whispered, smiling. "That reminds me . . ." She adjusted her black hair into a ponytail and removed her huge hoop earrings. "Just in case. I've had them ripped out before and it hurts like a bitch."

They entered through the door. As soon as they were inside, Peter could hear moaning. At first, he pictured something nasty involving the spicy zombie side dish and the magician.

"Great," he whispered. "Zombie sex."

Frowning, he felt his guts churn. He knew it happened, usually without the consent of the undead partner. They were helpless victims, desperately in need of a specialist social worker who could help prevent such abuses, sexual and otherwise.

During his various internships, he had seen enough to make him sick to his stomach. One family had accepted their deceased grandmother back into their home. Apparently, she had been too much for them to take care of, so they cut her arms and legs off and propped her in a child's seat in their kitchen, tossing her scraps once in a while. When he was there, she had her mouth duct-taped shut. He had called the cops. They had reluctantly come to take the zombie away, but they had let the family off the hook with a warning.

Now, they rounded a corner to see Smiley on the far side of a gray-brick room with a dirt floor. His lady friend was nowhere to be seen.

Peter and Ahlana stayed just out of sight.

"Kill," the magician yelled.

Peter looked to see who Smiley shouted at.

Two zombies—a three hundred-pound Samoan and a wiry white one with burn scars all over its naked back—had a pit bull cornered. The big corpse toppled onto the dog, which whimpered, crushed under the bloated weight.

Scrawny zombie kneeled down and rolled his partner out of the way before digging into the body of the smashed pit bull. His twisted fingers fought through the neck of the silent animal, which still kicked at the air. From the wound, the zombie pulled strips of red meat. Tendons snapped and coiled around his decaying hand. The dead man tentatively placed bloody pieces into his mouth, his face lighting up when the meat hit his tongue. He started with small bites, but quickly accelerated to shoveling full chunks down his throat.

The big guy sat up and didn't bother to rip pieces from the dead pet. He simply pulled the entire animal to his mouth. As he jabbed his discolored tongue hard into the dog's eye-socket, slurping out the insides, the skinny corpse got mad. He slapped at the Samoan's fat, tattooed arm and tried to steal the pit bull back.

"He's not doing the killing after all," Ahlana said. "He's training them to do it."

"You're not very stealthy, Ms. Demona," Smiley stated, rounding the corner.

"You fucking werewolf bitch!" Ahlana reached into her sweatshirt and pulled out an array of silver knives.

"Werewolf?" he asked, surprised. "I think I have had enough of both of you. Chuck! Pato! Show these two what it's like to be dead."

The skinny white zombie jumped to his feet and charged. Samoan stayed put, gorging himself on another bite of dog.

Peter backed into a corner. He hadn't been in a fight since fifth grade, when he had the tar kicked out of him by Ritchie Stevens, who then proceeded to steal his football cards. He watched from afar as Ahlana flashed a brilliant smile. The lanky zombie did the same, except his was missing teeth and filled with chunks of bloody fur.

Ahlana stepped forward and tossed her knife at the corpse. The butt end hit him on the forehead, leaving little more than a scratch before falling to the ground.

"Good shot." Smiley giggled, toying casually with the cufflinks on his fancy blue suit as he watched from the side.

"The knife was improperly balanced. Not my fault," Ahlana muttered.

Peter suddenly came to the conclusion he had made a bad decision. His new friend's confidence had blinded him to how much danger he was walking into. He wondered if Ahlana's monster killing abilities were enough to protect herself, let alone him. Realizing the door was a few feet away, he considered just taking off. That was the second time in a matter of hours he had thought of running away and he wasn't proud of the fact.

As the cloud of doubt in Peter's mind grew larger, Ahlana tossed a second knife. This time it slid into the corpse's skull, right between its eyes. A bit of blood seeped from the gash as the zombie collapsed. The cloud faded away.

One killer corpse was down. The other still toyed with the dog meat in the corner of the room.

Peter stared at the docile zombie, feeling safe.

When Ahlana yelled, "Watch out," he realized too late that Smiley had snuck up behind him. The magician shoved him onto the ground next to the pile of pit bull guts the massive corpse was feeding off of.

Peter kicked at the dirt to push himself out of the monster's reach, but he wasn't fast enough. The zombie wrapped his thick hand around Peter's ankle and pulled him in. Peter shrieked at the pressure on his leg. The cries were choked out when the corpse put his free hand around Peter's neck.

As he gasped for air, Peter watched Ahlana reach into her hoody and pull out a stake. She ran at the fat corpse and jumped onto his back. With frenzy in her eyes, she wrapped one arm around the dead man's neck and raised the stake to pound it through his brain. Before she could, the zombie leaned forward and took a huge bite out of Peter's neck.

Peter screamed and clutched at the tear in his flesh. Warm blood shot between his fingers, spraying everywhere.

The zombie's lunged, throwing Ahlana to the ground. A puff of dirt rose up on her impact. She sprang to her feet and grabbed the dead man's greasy black hair. Relentlessly, she pulled him away from Peter's throat. As she dragged him away, the fat corpse stuck his blood-covered tongue out, straining to catch more of the red liquid splashing all over the room.

With a quick shot, she pierced the zombie's thick nose with the stake, splitting one nostril and pushing the majority of the cartilage nub to the side. She held tight to the piece of wood, using it to stir. As she mashed the corpse's brains, its fingers shook. When they stopped moving, she stepped back and let the dead man fall.

Peter knew he wasn't succeeding at holding the blood in. He was losing focus. The absurdity of a zombie-rights activist being killed by the people he intended to protect crossed his mind. He reminded himself that it wasn't their fault. They were turned into weapons by Smiley. When a dog kills a person, it isn't the dog's fault, it's the owners. This situation was no different.

As Ahlana approached him, he forced a smile. He released it when he felt the blood dripping from his lips.

"I was starting to like you," Ahlana whispered.

Smiley interrupted the exchange. "You just come here and kill my friends? Do you really think you're doing any good for anyone? You fucking stupid humanitarians!"

Ahlana responded with a kick that sent the magician to the ground. She stood over him and sat down on his chest. Straddling him, she screamed in his face. With every word she yelled, she punched. Blood spurted up at her, getting all over her sweatshirt, which seemed to piss her off even more.

She ran her hands through Smiley's gelled hair, then clutched at it and used it to grip his head as she slammed the back of his skull against the ground again and again.

When the magician stopped kicking, she stood up.

Then she slid her heel into Smiley's skull through his eye and ground down with the back of her foot. Pulpy retina gurgled out of the hole. She repeated with his other eye.

"It's going to take me hours to get the brains off my shoe," she said, groaning.

It was the last thing Peter heard.

II.

Ahlana slammed the door to her apartment, kicked her bloody shoes off and went straight for her freezer.

"Shit," she said after a moment of pawing through frozen dinners, only to discover she had no ice cream. Instead, she reached into the cupboard and pulled out a box of individually wrapped brownies. She paced around, munching on chocolate and shaking her head.

As idealistic as Peter was, his heart had been in the right place. Plus, he was cute, particularly when he was getting insightful about the plight of dead folks.

"This is exactly why I need to keep to myself."

She ripped open the clear plastic sheath of another brownie and sat on her couch. Turning the TV on, she flipped through a couple channels, then turned it off again. She grabbed a book from the stack next to her couch and tried to read, but couldn't focus on the words. Her mind kept playing film of Peter's smile. The way it had crept onto his face one side at a time was so charming, even if his teeth weren't as white as she preferred.

She wondered if she would have been able to get him interested in her. Maybe he had been. Why else would he hang around?

Grunting, she tossed a throw pillow across the room.

Ahlana heard someone wander up the hall outside her door. She figured it was one of her neighbors, but it was three in the morning. The likelihood of any member of the contingent of elderly women that lived on her floor staying out past nine was extremely slim.

The shuffling of feet moved closer, then stopped.

When she opened the door and Peter's carcass wandered into her apartment, she wasn't terribly surprised.

"Hello, handsome," she said.

Peter moaned in response. His eyes wouldn't stay focused. They roamed from side to side, looking for something. Ahlana trailed behind him, amused, as he wandered through her apartment. In the doorway to her bedroom, he stopped and spent five minutes staring into the darkness as he ran his hand over the wall trying to find the light switch. When he found it and the light went on, he squinted, groaned and backed away.

Ahlana giggled.

Peter moved to the bathroom, where he was able to find the light switch immediately. Climbing into the tub, he turned the water on very warm. It went pink as it mingled with the blood leaking out of his throat.

"Okay. You can clean up, but you aren't going to sleep there. I'll put out a tarp or something," Ahlana said, moving out of the bathroom to dig through closets.

A few minutes later, Peter emerged, his clothes dripping pink water onto the red carpet.

"No! No! No! Get back in there!" Ahlana screamed.

Peter's head bounced around a bit, surprised at the noise. He backed up onto the linoleum.

"Well, this is going to be weird," she said, realizing she had to dry him off. "Can you at least take your own clothes off?"

In response, he lifted one arm out to the side and stared at her. After a couple seconds, his left eye drooped shut.

Ahlana looked down at her own clothes. Her sweatshirt was soaked in gore. A bit of skin clung to her shoulder and brownie crumbs covered her bosom. Surprisingly, her skirt was blood-free, as was the white tank top she wore underneath her hoody. She decided she might as well keep them clean.

"If you weren't dead, this would be so awkward." She removed her sweatshirt, then her skirt and tank top, until she stood in front of the corpse wearing only a bright green bra and matching panties. Pushing Peter's arms up over his head, she fought with his wet T-shirt to set him free. Then she tugged his soaked jeans down to his ankles and pulled his feet through one at a time. She left his boxers on.

As quickly as possible, she ran a black towel over her dead friend's cold flesh.

When she finished, she sat him on the floor. His legs pointed out in either direction, making him look somewhat childlike. Sitting directly in front of him, she said, "This is not the way I usually like to play nurse."

She wrapped his neck with gauze, for aesthetic purposes only. The wound wasn't going to heal and she knew it. As she did this, she felt something poking against her thigh. She looked down to see that the zombie had an erection.

"Oh, that is so not right," she groaned.

For a split second, she thought about it. After all, he was very fresh. With the bandages, the only thing that gave away his lack of life was his groaning and the way he had one eye opened and one closed. She felt a tingling in her groin.

Springing to her feet, she said, "No way. You go sit on the couch and chill out."

He obeyed and she went into her bedroom, closing the door behind her.

∏

When she opened her door the next morning, she was ready to pick up the paper and lounge around in her bathrobe all day. That was until she saw the headline: "Zombie Murders Continue."

She grabbed the phone.

"Dwight, you asshole! You said Smiley was responsible for these murders," Ahlana screamed.

"Did I? I thought I told you he was the lead werewolf and that the werewolves were behind it."

"Don't mess with me Dwight. Just because we had a fling doesn't mean I'm unwilling to jab some silver up your ass."

"Yeah, that's not all you want to jab up my ass," he snickered into the phone like a kid who had just discovered sex jokes. "Okay. I took advantage of you, but I was under orders. Babe, I didn't want him dead. Did you ever see his show? I saw him rip open a corpse's rib cage and a flock of doves carrying tulips in their beaks flew out. Doves with fucking tulips!"

"Why the hell did you tell me that then?" Ahlana took a seat on her couch next to Peter, who sat cross-legged, quietly humming something.

"That's a funny story, actually. You see, Smiley tried to use you to stop us, but I fooled you into stopping him. You're so gullible! I could probably tell you that the president is a werewolf and you'd believe me. I mean, the man's a werepig, which is like a distant cousin, but still . . ."

Ahlana kept her calm. "But why did you want each other killed?"

"Smiley had found out about us. He was worried that investigations into zombie murders would shine a light on his rinky-dink underground corpse fighting tournaments, which he made a nice bit of money off of. Dude should have known not to threaten fucking werewolves. As if we would back down for a magician. Ha!

"Anyway, I knew you would have a plan. Obviously you're alive, we're alive and Smiley's dead, so everybody's good, right?"

Ahlana looked at Peter and frowned. "Obviously," she said, hanging up the phone without giving any hint that everything was far from good.

"Well, honey, do you think you're up to killing people and eating their brains?"

Peter's neck creaked as he turned his head to face her. His humming stopped and he opened his jaw wide and closed his left eye. A quiet moan came from deep in his throat.

"That's cute, but we've got a lot of work to do."

Π

Ahlana built a dummy by stuffing a pair of jeans and a long-sleeve shirt with rags and hooking it together with duct tape. She had a watermelon that she would have preferred to eat, but she attached it to the dummy's neck instead. Then she pasted a picture of a werewolf to it and propped it up in the corner of the living room.

"Kill!" she yelled.

Peter remained on the couch. A bag of garbage in the corner of the kitchen had attracted his attention. He stared at it, quivering.

"Eat brains!"

"Destroy the werewolf!"

He finally got off of the couch, but ignored the dummy and went to the garbage.

Ahlana watched as he tore through the bag. She moved in to see what had freaked him out. Sticking out of the top was yesterday's newspaper, conveniently turned to a page with a big picture of James Smiley and a lengthy tribute to the man and his magic. She laughed.

"That's right. You hate him, don't you?"

Peter roared and scraped his fingers at the bag, spilling banana peels and empty jars of peanut butter onto the linoleum floor.

She went into her room and found an autographed head shot she got the first time she had gone to Smiley's show. At the time, she had thought he was a stud, so she bought everything he was selling. She later regretted the waste of money.

She took the werewolf picture off the dummy's melon and replaced it with the glossy photo of Smiley. "Hey tough guy, why don't you come get the real Smiley? Eat his fucking brains!"

Peter charged clumsily at the dummy and sunk his teeth into the melon. Ahlana watched with glee as his dead tongue ripped through the green shell and probed the juicy pink middle, sucking and slurping. He crushed the melon/skull in a matter of seconds.

"Stop," Ahlana ordered.

Peter kept gnawing.

"You're done!" Ahlana grabbed the picture and hid it behind her back.

Peter's jaw dropped open and a stream of pink goo filled with black seeds dripped out of his mouth. He swatted at her arm and lost his balance.

Ahlana tried to stop him from falling into her stereo, but wasn't quick enough. One zombie hand went through the black mesh of a speaker while the other pushed through the top of the CD player before the whole shelf toppled over, dumping a pile of discs onto Peter's head as he fell.

Ahlana groaned and helped her zombie to his feet.

Over the next three days, they continued the exercise, using inflated plastic bags rather than watermelons from then on. After the first few times, she put the picture of the werewolf beneath the picture of Smiley. Then she put it above the picture of Smiley.

Eventually, she removed the picture of the magician altogether and just used the picture of the werewolf. She was happy to see that Peter still attacked with as much ferocity as he originally intended for his zombie-rights-abusing nemesis.

To further incent him to munch on brains, she decided not to feed him.

∏

Ahlana woke to the grating beeps spewing out of her alarm clock. She slid into a bathrobe and walked out to say good morning to Peter.

"Hey!" she yelled at him instead.

Bits of yellow foam stuffing hung from his mouth. He turned to look at her innocently, slowly climbing down from the mess of torn upholstery and visible springs he had turned her couch into.

She ran into her room and grabbed a football helmet that a guy had left there once. Coercing it over Peter's head, she fastened the chinstrap. He slapped at the hard plastic and groaned. "Don't fight it, sugar.

The face guard will stop you from filling your belly with junk food and spoiling the big meal."

Things like this and the destruction of her stereo made Ahlana realize that Peter's ideals hadn't been so crazy. She could see how frustration might lead to abuse, especially since Peter wouldn't fight back at all.

The idea of a social worker that specialized in zombies was a good one. Hopefully, it didn't go down the tubes with her friend's life. She wondered if it was something she could do. Then she reminded herself that she killed monsters. That was her calling.

After eating a bowl of cereal while Peter watched and whined, she went into her armory. Staring at the piles of weapons, she wondered what she could give Peter to make him more destructive. "Come here," she yelled.

He paused for a moment and tilted his head to the side, then got up and joined her in the room.

"Good zombie."

She handed him a baseball bat. Clumsily, he clutched it with both hands. He swung it around slowly, and then knocked himself on the head before dropping it.

"What if I tape it to your hands?" She asked.

Peter didn't answer. He just stared around the room, swaying as if barely able to stand up. For a moment, Ahlana doubted whether he would be of any value at all and contemplated leaving him at home.

"Well, if I were you, I would love the opportunity to lick the brains out of the fellas that made me turn into a walking corpse. So what do you want to use to crack skulls?"

She watched as Peter fell to his knees and crawled around the room, pawing through weapons. He came upon the power drill. Pulling the trigger, his eyes lit up as he watched the bit spin. Ahlana wasn't fast enough to stop him from sinking it into his forearm, which caused him to shake his head back and forth quickly and drop the drill. After a moment, he must have realized it didn't hurt, because he picked the weapon back up and stared at it again.

"So, that's the one you like, huh?"

She knelt down beside him and grabbed a roll of duct tape. Pulling his hand onto her lap, she placed the drill against his knuckles. Using a healthy wad of tape, she adjoined corpse and machine.

Peter put his free hand on top of hers.

"Don't be a weirdo, zombie," she said, pushing his hand away.

When the weapon was attached solidly enough, she stood up. Peter shook his hand. His mouth turned to a frown and he made a buzzing sound.

"Don't worry. We'll turn it on when we need to," Ahlana purred reassuringly.

She grabbed a couple rubber bands, took Peter by his leash, and left her apartment.

During her years as a monster hunter, she had learned that the most efficient way to find anyone or anything was simply to watch and follow.

As they drove to Dwight's place, night filtered down and squeezed into all the city's cracks and crevices. They made their way through the streets lined with brown brick buildings and dirty gutters. Ahlana glanced at Peter in the passenger seat and thought about what could have happened. He wasn't her typical guy; not flashy or metro. The man was good looking in a generic way, but he was smart. That was cool. And he had that smile.

Now, of course, he didn't really smile so much as grimace. At best, his lips twitched up coincidentally and formed a wide, toothy grin. It was far from charming. Not to mention that grunts and groans didn't make for intelligent conversation.

When they arrived at Dwight's house, it blew her mind that, after a few minutes of waiting, their target waltzed out nonchalantly, not even checking over his shoulder. Sure, he had no reason to believe she was going to follow him, but he was a fucking werewolf for Christ's sake. Shouldn't some precaution be utilized? Most people would notice a big black cargo van following them for a few miles, even at a couple blocks distance, but not Dwight.

Ahlana knew he wasn't the smartest werewolf to ever howl at the moon, but this surprised her. He didn't even bother to park far away and sneak into his destination. Instead, he pulled right in front of the big brick building and swaggered in without a care.

Ahlana looked at the sign and kicked herself for not thinking of it on her own. "The Independent Art Institute of Milwaukee," she read out loud.

She parked the van behind

Dwight's car.

Inside, the clicking of her heels echoed over the brown tiles that lined the hallway. Peter marched slowly behind her. Most rooms were dark and empty, so it wasn't hard to follow the sound to the one that was in use.

Standing just outside the door, Ahlana took a couple deep breaths. She tried to meet Peter's eyes, but they refused to focus on her.

After removing the faceguard from his helmet, she looked at him and moved her face closer. She put her hands on the sides of his head and went in for a kiss. His chomping teeth sent her lips in another direction. She left a purple lipstick print on the front of his helmet instead.

"Let's get 'em, tiger," she said, wrapping the rubber band tight around the trigger of Peter's hand-mounted drill.

She flung open the door and unzipped her sweatshirt, taking it off to reveal thick shoulder straps that held her arsenal. Under the straps, she wore a tight lycra body suit, ink black. She pulled out a metal baseball bat that was tucked between the straps on her back, pounded it against the tile floor and said, "Let's go, bitches!"

"We're cool, babe. Don't do this," Dwight pleaded. Behind him, a dozen students stood in front of easels coaxing hideous modern art from their brushes. Half of them ran out of the room screaming. Ahlana let them pass.

"We are so not cool," she replied, tightening her grip on the bat. "I should have done this the first time I saw you."

Zombie Peter pushed past her and groaned as he flailed his drill arm. He had the bit ripping through Dwight's temple before the ex-boyfriend could wolf out.

As his body hit the floor, the remaining students tossed their art to the side. The room filled with growls as their flesh bubbled up. Fur pushed to the surface as bones cracked and bodies reshaped. One student with a particular flair for the dramatic dropped to his knees. He clutched his lengthening wolf claws to the side of his twisting face as his jaws extended and a howl burst from between the fangs. Upon completion of the change, he did a few neck rolls and stood up, spreading his arms in an attack position.

The teacher nodded and took a seat behind his desk as his students roared at the intruders. In wolf form, the teacher's hair was a bizarre strawberry blonde, excessively long and well-groomed.

Peter went straight for the drama queen werewolf. The beast swung at the zombie's head. Ahlana cringed at the sound of the wolf's paw slapping the football helmet, but the strike didn't faze Peter. He ducked and gnawed at the creature's fur-covered belly, drilling into the side of its ribs at the same time. Blood trickled from the wolf's stomach and squirted out of the drill hole.

As Peter pulled away with a chunk of furry meat clenched between his teeth and drops of viscera falling from his dead chin, Ahlana moved in and crushed the skull of one of the wolves. She smiled at the piece of animal brain that stuck to the sweet spot of her bat.

Another fur ball jumped her from behind. She felt its dank breath as its fangs neared her neck. They stopped short and the beast's grip loosened after she jabbed a silver tipped stake under his rib cage. She figured she had punctured a lung from the way the wolf's breathing turned raspy and a geyser of blood launched from his mouth.

Ahlana moved on to her third wolf. Pulling throwing stars from her weapon strap, she noticed Peter was in trouble. His arm was being twisted behind his back by a large, black-haired wolf. She tossed a star that grazed the beast's ear, but didn't stop him from biting down on the zombie's bicep. Once its teeth had sunk deep into the already dead flesh, the monster shook its head from side to side, eventually snapping the bone. The wolf gnawed through the remaining strands of tendon and muscle that held the arm on before tossing Peter's limb to the side of the room.

Ahlana grinned as the wolf stepped away. It must have thought the fight was over. Peter apparently thought otherwise. He raised his weapon and let the gleaming steel bit burrow into the monster's eye. The werewolf howled and backed up, giving the zombie room to pounce. Peter lunged and sunk his teeth into the monster's throat. Fresh blood spurted all over the white football helmet.

After Ahlana tossed a throwing star into one of the few remaining wolf's skulls, she watched as Peter ripped out gristly werewolf burger and spat it to the floor in chunks until he got down to the animal's spinal cord. At that point, he stood up and licked the blood from his lips.

The art room floor was a mess. Incomplete abstracts on canvas were covered with smears of green and blue paint. On top of this lay the bloody corpses of the students, which had reverted back to their human forms after death. All that remained was the leader.

"Now that was just pointless bloodshed," he said, standing up behind his desk. "You're still going to die."

"Wait," Ahlana screamed. "Why are you doing this? What did killing those people and blaming zombies have to do with making art?"

The wolf shrugged. "The two are not related. We are wolves. We eat flesh by nature. Hiding that fact is imperative to the success of our art scheme."

The flesh on the teacher's belly peeled to the side, leaving a gaping black hole. Green stalks tentatively poked out. Slowly, they crawled over the desk. "I am the werewolf god!" His shouting sounded like hundreds of voices layered over each other.

Ahlana stared as the tentacles moved toward her and Peter. Immediately, her mind rolled back to that day in the swamp. Her body froze, thinking about the way the swamp creature's tentacles had destroyed her man's face. Eight tentacles had crawled out of that bayou creature's mouth.

She counted eight squirming out of the dark chasm in the werewolf god's abdomen, each covered with convulsing blue veins that bulged under the surface. She almost laughed at how slowly these ones moved. Taking a knife from her sash, she tossed it at one of them. The proboscis flipped to the side quickly, avoiding the blade, which landed uselessly on the tile floor.

As if in recognition of the threat, the tentacles picked up speed. One wrapped around Ahlana, pinning her arms to her side and pushing her against the wall. The werewolf god simply watched and laughed.

Peter, with the little speed he possessed as a zombie, had no chance. The stalks wrapped around his torso and lifted him into the air. He kicked his legs and flopped his head from side to side. If it weren't for the chinstrap, he would have shaken his helmet loose. He snapped his jaws at the writhing tentacles, but they moved too quickly and he ended up chomping at air instead. Jamming the spinning drill bit on his remaining hand into the coil of tentacle that was squishing his midsection only resulted in a few drops of thick blue fluid falling to the floor, where they blended in with the other smears of paint and gore.

The werewolf god hissed as one of the many free tentacles tore off Peter's drill arm. It flung the severed limb into the black hole in its belly, which sighed as it received the treat. He repeated this with both of the zombie's legs.

"I prefer fresh meat over these cold cuts." The beast chuckled, dropping Peter's torso.

The werewolf god flicked his tentacles over Ahlana's smooth skin. She tried to push herself free as the thing squirmed over her flesh, leaving a trail of slime across her latex suit as it moved down to caress her groin.

"That's right. Dwight told me about your little defect. I think I'll remove that particular limb last."

"This art fucking sucks!" was all Ahlana could think to yell as the tentacles closed in on her.

The wolf was taken aback enough that Ahlana could slip a lycra coated arm free from its grip. She grabbed one of her knives and sliced completely through the thick limb that had captured her. As a stream of the thick blue ooze splattered across her face, she unraveled herself from the limp tentacle.

The wolf screamed as Ahlana grabbed her bat. Swinging wildly, she made her way to Peter's torso. She dropped the weapon and grabbed the back of his shirt, lifting him up.

"You know what to do, sweetie," she whispered before throwing him headfirst at the monster's face. Like a zombie torpedo, Peter flew across the room. Upon impact, his teeth sunk into the wolf's face. He clamped onto the animal's forehead and hung. The beast wrapped his paws around Peter and pulled, but the corpse's bite was relentless.

Ahlana followed the bite attack with a series of blows from the baseball bat, sending the self-proclaimed wolf god to the ground. His tentacles fluttered aimlessly. She smashed each of them to a pile of green and blue mush. They looked like gummy worms that had been caught in the sun, dried up and trampled underfoot.

She bashed until she could detect no more movement.

"Why don't you let go now, sweetie," she said to Peter, who still gnawed on the wolf's face.

He looked up at her, his lips sloppy with blood. Through the muck, that smile emerged, starting on one side before slowly shuffling over to the other. Wiggling his body, he attempted to move toward her. Instead, his awkward motions sent him falling through the hole in the wolf's stomach.

Ahlana tried to grab him, but wasn't quick enough.

"Fuck!" She screamed, whipping the baseball bat across the room. It clanged against the brick wall.

"Get a grip, babe. He was just a zombie," she said as she paced around, trying not to slip on the mélange of slimes and oozes that coated the floor. After a moment, she decided she didn't want to see Peter die twice.

"This is the stupidest thing I've ever done, Peter!" she yelled into the wolf chasm. It felt odd to say his name. She realized she hadn't done so since he had gone zombie.

Grabbing the most in-tact of the limp tentacles, she got a good grip and jumped into the hole.

"Peter!" she yelled, holding tight to the slippery makeshift rope.

She heard his moaning nearby as her eyes adjusted to the darkness. In the thin stream of light that seeped in from the hole above, she could make out piles of severed limbs. She focused on an elderly-looking hand that rose out of the mass, its twisted pointer finger gripped by the pudgy digits of a baby. Neither twitching limb was attached to a body.

Ahlana looked around some more and spotted Peter hanging by his teeth from another tentacle a few feet away. She kicked and kicked, swinging toward him. When she got close enough, she spread her legs and caught Peter's torso between her thighs.

As she climbed back out of the hole, zombie in tow, she muttered, "The things I'll do for a cute guy."

Peter moaned.

Ahlana looked down at the corpse. A sheet of glistening crimson covered a pale face, showing the first signs of rot. She decided to take back the cute part.

"Enjoy that position, because it's the closest you're going to get," she teased as they emerged from the stomach of the wolf.

She grabbed one of the dead student's backpacks. Dumping it out, she giggled at the mix of art history texts and wrinkled adult magazines that fell to the floor.

She stuffed Peter into the bag and put it on her back so his head poked out the top and faced the opposite direction. Smiling, she said, "We make quite a team. Don't we, honey?"

Peter gnashed his teeth in response.

The Man Who Flirted With Mother Nature

by
Mike Philbin

It was a very normal Spring day in the centre of Oxford. My eyes were streaming and my throat tickled from the abundance of wind-blown pollen in the air as I strolled through the crowds of Cornmarket Street. Nothing too sinister there. Trees pulsated with sun-ripened life. One or two leafy remnants of winter scurried about at the wind's behest.

The Spring sun shone proudly in the topaz sky and wisps of whimsical cloud were silently ushered away by a warm south-westerly breeze. Buds blossomed in this gracefully undulating cascade of light and shade. Flowers rippled in the warm current. Pigeons pecked at crumbs outside KFC. I continued my lunchtime stroll, heading out northwards past Tolkein's *Eagle & Child*.

I suddenly started to see things as they really were—a student and his friend sniffed at a holly bush, a woman in a grey pinstripe dress suit crouched beside a bed of daffodils, a young girl rested her behind against a tree trunk, the sun tiptoeing gaily across her bright, smiling face.

If you looked again.

The student's head was buried in the holly bush, he pulled back a lunatic face studded with shimmering specks of blood. He frantically waved his friend to try this. His friend didn't want to but the student took hold of the back of his skull and thrusts his face into the holly bush, there was a muffled shriek of panic and cry of pain then a groan of pleasure. The student pushed his face over the shoulder of his friend so that both their faces were buried in the thorny bush. If you listened carefully, you could hear the greasy red berries tittering camply as the student pressed forward with all his weight, kissing his friend on the ear lobe before reaching round and unzipping his friend's fly and unfurling his cock. Pulling on it frantically until creamy white milk spilled out onto lethal leaves. If you looked at the leaves, looked real close, saw that vaginal pores had opened up on the leathery surface of the holly leaves and were soaking up the spermy goodness. I blinked in confusion. That couldn't have happened.

The woman in the grey pinstriped dress suit was about 50 years old, very well presented. She'd crouched down; if you looked again, she'd knelt down in the flower bed like a supplicant at the altar. Her 15 denier slate-grey knees were soaked. As she bent over to sniff at the daffodils, the pinstriped skirt of her dress suit pulled tight like the one that pulled tight over Jackie's ass as she clambered across the trunk of JFK's brain-strewn limo. Her thin, pink tongue was out, a clear line of spittle depended from the end of it. Below, the gaping mouth of the daffodil waited for the spittle thread to snap. There was a really pungent musk coming off the pairing, the sickly sweet smell of carved open Spanish sausages. Her spittle poured into the daffodil's gaping maw. The business woman bowed down further and took a bite out of the head of the still munching daffodil. She chewed on the flower and a gallon more spittle spilled onto the gaping maws of neighbouring daffodils, all their heads stretched up to bathe in her gobby benediction. She looked around momentarily and I could see she no longer had teeth at the front. Her teeth had dissolved, nerve endings dangling from the raw red holes in her gums. She returned to her feeding.

The young girl resting against the tree. I couldn't even watch the vicious rape she seemed totally oblivious to; her body was jolted by the ferocity of the assault about ten times per heartbeat and she betrayed no discomfort. A glass-eyed street sweeper in regulation yellow vinyl coveralls wandered by half-awake, his street sweeping brush at a lethargic tilt, and she just managed a girlish wave at him. He watched gore-spattered bark-stripped 'penises' pile-drive in and out of her female orifice. Her jeans and T-shirt all tore open at the back. A branch reached round her face and poured oozing white sap in her mouth, up her nose, in her eyes—and she fuckin' loved it.

The street sweeper could no longer resist the lure. His rough fists clenched and he ran over at full tilt, his work boot aimed at her heaving chest—it connected with her fragile sternum and she let out a spluttering red sigh of erotic torture. The street sweeper punched at her chest until the blood from his smashed knuckles mixed with the blood pouring out of her split sternum. When he still could get no purchase with his bare hands, he took out his pocket knife and carved his way through her flesh to get to her ribs. He pulled a few ribs off so that he could get his fists around the exposed sternum. He was pulling away at the breast bone like a man possessed, one work boot up on the tree, until the breast bone suddenly broke open like a soiled coffin lid revealing the pulsating heart and the quivering lungs. All the time her face was a sun-drenched mask of overpowering ecstasy. A nauseating stench belched out from her gaping chest wound—not a stench of the war trenches, not a stench of the slaughter house, but something much more aggressive and insidious; the stench of purest lust. I don't know how I resisted the gory debauch, how I didn't pour my worthless muzzle into her erotic dog bowl of richest red.

I shook my head.

I had moved down the road before it even dawned on me to look back over my shoulder . I never got to execute even that most basic function. A grave force, an unfathomable power, an uncanny attraction pulled me on towards ultimate consequence. I staggered along in a drunken dance, my head was close to exploding, my eyes throbbing in their sockets. Heading back into central Oxford where the traffic jams were still inertia bound. Long lines of cars going nowhere, that's the Oxford we all knew, the Oxford we all loved. But this time, the cars really were going nowhere, their drivers and passengers having long since abandoned their metal friends to the flowery delirium.

The centre of Oxford had ground to a halt.

I can't believe I actually thought about going back to work. The Earth was truly coming to an end for mankind and I was actually thinking that some insane knowledge could be gleaned from a quick visit to my usual shortlist of news websites before 'websense' cut off our access at 2 PM sharp. Could anything really tell me any more than I'd already witnessed all around me? Surely the 'net would contain only Yesterday's News *forever*. Surely that was the end of headline writing. Surely all the journalists in the world had just been made redundant.

I couldn't work out how I'd been spared.

Maybe there was a very important reason I'd been spared this horrific assimilation into Mother Nature's plentiful bosom. I tell you what though, it fucking hurt like hell to watch it and wonder what ecstasies I was missing out on, despite the traumatic imagery. Maybe there would be an extra chapter written in the *Book of Earth's Demise* just for me, the way *Revelations* was welded onto the backend of the Christian Bible. Surely, there had to be some ulterior motive why myself (and others like me?) hadn't been subsumed into the epileptic fracture in HER insatiable libido.

But of course it was obvious. There had to be others like me out there whom this curse hadn't crushed flat. The revelation was tinged with regret as I really wanted to join my fellow man in his aching moment of annihilation-by-sex. I yearned for obliteration.

I used to think I, the non-theist, was the one who was awake. The one with open eyes staring blankly in the face of man's theological folly. The one ruled by logic and reason, not blinkered by theology, not crippled by superstition. Suddenly I realised I had been trapped in a tumour of time and space like Sleeping Beauty locked in her castle of thorns. Would there be someone to awaken me with a kiss? I couldn't even remember the last time I'd taken a breath.

Was I still even alive? The centre of town was so quiet; usually Cornmarket Street, or any of its sixteenth century arteries, was saturated with the sounds of shoe heals and baby screams and mindless chatter of scientific, political or merely domestic import. Today, all the learned inhabitants were lost in the most extreme expression of human existence and I was a scowling corpse propped up at the gory disco.

I found a bench and sat among the mayhem for I don't know how long.

I checked my pulse to make sure I was still alive. I could have died and passed on to another realm, there was no ruling out such craziness. I mean how does one tell the difference between one reality and another? 'If you prick us, do we not bleed?' applied to either side of the great divide. As if through a dissolving filter, I heard the field martens chirping high in the sky above their nests. The wind caressed the cherry blossom. Harmless insects alighted upon my thighs.

It was just another normal day for Mother Nature, right?

A mating couple toppled towards me spilling their maggoty ejaculate in every direction and the sight of it only added to my exhaustion—I was beyond revulsion. I now only felt pity for these creatures. Their fragile skulls cracked against the concrete armrest of my bench and something landed on my lap like the promise of an imminent downpour. The glob of juice embedded in my thigh and took root—that day every spilled ounce would flourish. But not on me. I watched the hopeful parasite quickly wither and die on my thigh; dead petals crumbled to the floor. I brushed their desiccated pollen off my office trousers and got up. I could take no more of this torture. I was going to be a part of this big fuck. I'd decided to throw caution to the wind. I'd decided I was going out in a ball-roasting blaze of sexual glory.

Her, she'd do.

She had the glazed look of someone who'd already been part-fucked into a stupor. I couldn't even be certain she was wholly human. Once I penetrated this thing, it could be any thorny abomination between the folds of her lips. But my dander was up. I thought, 'I'm gonna fuck this thing then I'm gonna find another just like her and fuck that too. And keep on going until natural wear and tear, or the horrors of meeting a fully Transformed one, takes its toll.' I'd resolved to fuck and fuck and fuck like a dingo until I was a dried husk expunged of all its sexual essence, drained of vital juices.

But the look in her eyes. She didn't even see me. I could feel every twitch and shudder of her multiple-orgasming sexual obituary but her glassy eyes beheld another. A distant lover captivated her. She had on that thousand yard stare of grunts in the Vietnam rain forest. Sure, it was a good, physical fuck, my load was shot, but is that all there is to life?

I zipped up and sorta wandered off in no general direction. I felt sorta guilty. No not guilty, just empty—an unresolved creation, a yet to be. What was a physical but invisible

4

creature like me to do? How was I now expected to pass my time? Was there a normal world, a human oasis, on some isolated part of this planet as yet untouched by the Transformation. It was just the most haunted situation imaginable. Those of them that were basically still human in form wandered about looking for other things to fuck or be fucked by; other non-human things. I bumped into one or two of them deliberately just to see what would happen, copped a feel too while I was at it. I mean, why not. Amused myself a bit. Committed no great sin. The no-longer-humans, they were the real sin—when you disturbed them from their torpor they moved their mouths like fuck-doll chickens in some nest of wanting. Slow, deliberate opening and closing that said, "Here's where I want it, right in my fucking mouth."

It struck me. The true horror. Worse than all the scenes of anatomical debauch. Much worse than Mother Nature having her fun. Much worse than the dead look in lost eyes. The very worst thing about today was this simple fact—man was fucked.

The sky grew morose.

You pass these un-people in crowded streets, you expect to hear some grunts, some groans, a cough, a gossamer wisp of gossip, intrigue, interest. But there was none of that. A mouth might fall open spilling saliva down its front. A body might swing round in your direction. Sexual anatomy might twitch in the hope you're one of them. But this one was different. I heard him before I saw him. He was doing all the right things, all the human things, all the grunting and groaning and swearing; he was swearing through a hoarse throat and a ragged beard. He was still fully human but he had gone berserk with his situation. He just couldn't take it any more. It was too much of an assault upon all he held dear. He slid about in the middle of a congregation of these un-things, swinging a razor sharp samurai sword, carving up wave after wave of them. Grunting and snarling as he hefted his arc of steel. Had I seen him before, in between destinations maybe? Before the Transformation? Did I remember him striding down the streets of Oxford in his rotting T-shirt in all weathers, his mangled hair swirling about his head? He was a big bloke with a big beer belly. But he didn't look like a Goliath; he looked like a terrified little creature despite his stature.

I couldn't take my eyes off him. He was sweating like a pig. How long had he been at it? He'd carve off a limb of one of the un-things and flowers would grow in the stump. He'd decapitate another and a burst of spinning seeds would explode from the falling carcass. These seeds would stick into anything within their blast radius; grow there, grow anywhere, anywhere a seed could stick. Those that stuck into the giant sword-wielding berserker sprouted weakly then crumbled and died. And then I knew. Another just like me.

I shouted across to him, 'Hey!'

He instantly stopped scything through the waves of non-humans. Stood there with his sword held out in one hand. His big shoulders lifted up and down. His eyes darted about. His snarl softened. Sweat poured from him. He had heard a human voice. One wrong move . . . one wrong move and I'd be sliced in two like all those at his feet.

I don't remember what I did to calm him. I did keep repeating, 'We are the only two humans . . . We are the only two humans . . . ' I could have said any random thing as long as I made him understand I was still a human being. He seemed mesmerised by my voice. Any voice would have the same impact. His fat arms were swollen red from swinging that sword about all afternoon. Amazingly, I was able to ease the weapon from his vice-like grip and only once he was disarmed did he truly calm down. The intricately carved bone and ray skin handle was boiling hot and slick with sweat.

We ended up in a café. I say a café. It used to be a high-class French café-style franchise before the rutting juices and budding new offspring of Mother Nature's latest experiment redecorated the place.

'Our children will understand how to deal with all this better than us.' My words were meant to convince him but they were applicable to myself, too. We'd smashed the front off a coke machine and helped ourselves to the still-chilled cans inside. He was still trembling. His eyes bulged from his face whenever one of the lusty creatures bumped into our window smearing all sorts of greasy discharge along it.

'I tried everything to rid the world of that filth.' He sulked at his coke.

I wondered how long this insane world event had been going on. For us, here in Oxford, it had been the one day. The first afternoon of the Transformation. How long had Mother Nature rampaged across the globe?

∏

And, you know, as mad as life had become we could have gone on living like that. Me and my beautiful brute of a friend; the only human left on planet Earth and I. There were factories and shops all over the world to raid. An inexhaustible supply of towels, bed linen, toilet paper, burger beef, bottled water and soda pop. We could reside in penthouse suites of all the best hotels free of charge. Dress like kings. Every meal a royal banquet. That was my dream. We could ride all the taxis and buses and trains (well, drive them, or learn how to) in the world. Could we even fly corporate jets from continent to continent? How fucking mad would that be?

But our pally paradise lasted only one day.

We hadn't even moved out of the broke-open café. The samurai sword still trembled between us, begging one of us to swipe it into their sweaty palm and smite down the other with its blood-keen edge. He was completely docile by then and he had this guilty little smirk on his face. As if he was about to say, 'What the Hell, there's nobody left who can judge me.' Might as well have it done with. That's what his face was saying. He looked out the window at the flora-sexual nightmare that continued to grind on in its sickening fashion. He smiled. He was about to offload some huge confession. That's what I saw in his eyes.

I put my hand on his—the size difference was terrifying; it was like a child stroking a bear paw. One tear rolled down his blood and shit and piss-caked face. Holy God, did I need to hear this now? Did I need to be shown some twisted aspect of my new (and only) friend that would tear our rocky relationship apart even before it started?

'You don't need to do this now.' I looked at his silver wrist watch. The minute hand no longer ticked out the minutes of our lives. All was still. Frozen.

'He was only eight or nine years old. I was just out of the army; what did I know? He was sat there like a lovely little cherub in pyjamas watching some film I had on. I remember heads coming off and screaming villagers; horsemen were rampaging through the gun smoke swinging heavy scimitars. I had my, you know, my dick in my hand. I was close, so close to spilling my load. I didn't even really remember he was still there, he was so enthralled. Then I realised he'd been watching me the whole time. I'll confess, I'm not the least well endowed person in the world. But you know what, that cute little kid with the Superman kiss curl on his freckled forehead was a double-handed delight. I made him do it again and again, despite his tears. Every time I babysat for my drunken sister. I didn't give a shit how it might affect the young 'un. Didn't care if my mental scarring of this crying, snivelling kid would ever heal.

Who would leave such a monster like me in charge of a vulnerable little kid like that?'

The samurai sword wanted his blood more than anything. I could see the mountain tops scintillating with the urge to virtually leap up at his beardy chin and insinuate itself across his wretched jugular. It knew what I had to do. I must kill this kiddy fiddler right now. Be the justice he so desperately demanded. But, you know what, I didn't take my chance. I just removed my hand from his. I think I muttered something like, 'Man was born to make mistakes,' and drained my can of coke. Something really trite like that. Man was born to make amends.

Then we went on to raid some convenience store nearby.

In the morning I had the nastiest hangover and he was no more. I hadn't heard him pack up his things and leave. I'm not sure I would have allowed it. There were no signs of a struggle in the neighbouring area, no blood trail that might lead to his decapitation. I still had the samurai sword. In fact it didn't want to leave my grasp. We were both comforted by the closeness. It was all that remained of our brief encounter. Listen to me, I sound as mad as he was.

Then it struck me. He confessed. He shared his sin with another. I sat there last night and listened to this brutal fuck confess how he tortured some little kid for his own sick release. It wasn't the crime that had taken him but the confession of the crime.

How did I know?

7

Well, I didn't really know but I suspected that to be the case. I envisioned some last scene of the hulking, lumbering fool attracted to the lure of a pollen hole, crunching thorns through his bewildered eyeballs and pouring tendrils of sticky green down his throat and his cock drilling down into the ground like a tri-furcated root system until he too was subsumed into the greater orgasmic good. I knew this, I suspected it to be true at least, because confession (whether religious or patri-monial) is something I'd never done. I'd heard lots of stories, listened to lots of confessions, nodded my head like a good doggy and never shared their revelations with another living soul.

Could that really be what *saved* me?

∏

Four months later and Mother Nature's persistence was becoming too great. I saw myself standing in the centre of Oxford, a town I was finding it impossible to leave, and just confessing all to God and the birds and the plants and the insects or any living thing that cared to listen. I heard myself confessing my crimes against my fellow man. I heard myself expunging myself of all the secrets people had told me: their affairs, their stealing, their sex crimes, their ambitions, their regret. Would such a release have really solved my conundrum, healed my torment?

One can never be sure of one's theories or beliefs.

I walked down Blue Boar Street overgrown with Mother Nature's perfumed jewellery of roots and fronds and budding petals. She was a planetary-sized seductress in all the right ways and that had become the sum total of my dilemma. I liked the way she was with me. I sensed her pussy willow branches dipping down to tease me as I passed beneath her. I sensed her sluttish flower heads reaching up to meet my lips. I sensed her sting of pollen begging me to succumb. But I refused her blatant sexual advances. Just out of sheer determination. I refused to be subjugated by her need for Transformation. I refused her passion, as painful as that was.

I have, so far, remained faithful to my human race.

Sex, Lies, Religion

by
Micci Oaten of Paparazzi Whore

Sex is the most natural instinct that you will ever feel throughout your entire life. Religion tries to control this, with catastrophic consequences.

As a child I was deeply curious about religion, mainly because I have members of my family who live their lives through it. My mother never encouraged me either way, saying it was my own choice. I was drawn, even that young, to wonder why people wanted to live their lives through any kind of belief that had been set out by another.

Every Sunday I would attend Sunday School, read my bible, listen to the vicar at our local church. Maybe the curiosity set in when I was christened at the age of 6 months; maybe it was imprinted and felt comforting like being close to my grandmother. Religion was a strong part of my childhood.

Then the hormones started to surge. Hitting my teens became very confusing. I believed, because of what I had observed and been told by others, that how I was feeling was wrong, and yet in my heart it felt so right. What was I to do? I was being torn in two.

As the years rolled by, my eyes opened even wider. I realised, even people who exhibited no sign of being religious and who never attended church had all these opinions and rules, opposing them and judging others.

'I just think it's wrong,' they would say, not really knowing how they came to their conclusion in the first place.

When you are born you are a blank canvas and a sponge, absorbing your surroundings and the people around you, watching their every move so that you can copy and 'fit in'.

The bullying in my teens became incredible. I was a 'lemon', a 'freak'—any kind of word that teenagers could throw at me with a punch. Where do you think they heard this opinion to make it their own? From adults around them who had not opened their eyes to break the chain of prejudice.

I do not remember reading in the Bible

that you should kick the crap out of anybody who is different to you. It has always been a backward approach to any situation showing a serious lack of intelligence.

I used to wear, throughout my teens, a small gold cross on a chain and people often asked me, 'Are you religious?' I would say, 'Hmm, maybe,' because at that point my eyes were becoming wider and wider to all the misery caused by the use of religious books.

But are religious books really to blame? I have come to the conclusion that they are not. It's the interpreters. They are interpret the books to use as tools to control human emotion and to keep people in line.

When anything is put into print, it naturally includes somebody's view and should therefore be questioned: Do you believe this is right or wrong? What do YOU believe? The main fault of many people is that they do not question anything at all, whether it's in the Bible, on the pages of a magazine or idle gossip. They take

everything at face value and live in fear of standing out with their view, even though there might be others who are just waiting for someone to have the balls to say it out loud.

'Well it must be true! It's in print or so and so told me' is what most say.

I am a bisexual woman and there is nothing I or anyone else can do about it. It's a fact.

When my band took part in the BBC TV show *Singing with the Enemy*, we were living with a religious band for a week. Their guitarist said on camera: 'I had a friend who *was* gay. He found God and He cured him.' Cured him? Of what? Being himself? Being who he truly is?

You cannot dictate a person's emotions. The frustrations of suppressing 'you' will turn into hatred of yourself, which will have a knock-on effect to others around you, as they will feel the brunt of your anger.

Is this what the Bible was created to do? I wonder why they didn't show this ridiculous comment on the show? Maybe because I was meant to be the bad person in the house and the religious band were the good guys who do or say nothing wrong.

What I learnt from them is that they believe loving the same sex is wrong and should be stopped. Their opinion is out of date. Our society is moving on. More and more people openly talk about them-selves sexually and are encouraged to be proud of who they are. Maybe this is why so many people are against war as they do not have a thirst to vent frustrations that are no longer there.

To love is not wrong. To have sex is not wrong. How can an emotion that makes you feel contented inside be wrong? Life throws enough crap at us, so why damn ourselves when we feel happy?

How you interpret the Bible describes how you feel about yourself and exposes you emotionally. If you have issues then you will use the book to attack others with. If, on the other hand, you have no issues then you will see the book as a guide and not a dictatorship.

The Bible has been used through the centuries to manipulate others to gain land, money or anything else that people want. This turns people's lives into a nightmare of bloodshed and loss. Power- hungry people promote the fear of us all 'burning in hell' and claim God is on their side, so that we will fight for the land, losing our lives for their want.

The main problem with the Bible and all other religious books is that they are all in the wrong hands—the hands of Man.

Camille O'Sullivan: Trickery Or Magic?

by Patti Plinko

very night before Houdini's great escape, his assistant would kiss him before he entered the water tank. On the tip of her tongue lay a key.

On March 27th, I was looking for escape; I went to see Camille O'Sullivan. Now as much as I'm told that to place another artist upon a pedestal leaves one in grave danger, it really is quite out of my hands. It's just a switch in your brain—and bam! It happens. One minute you are just watching, and then the next: Click! Snap! From nowhere they are 10,000ft above your head. Once up there you can't just reach on tiptoes and bring them back. The only thing to float down is realisation of the inevitable, because, at some point, that pedestal will reach such heady heights the artist starts to experience difficulty breathing. Nausea and giddiness kick in, then *Oop la la!* they come crashing down—Bam! And who do they land on?

Standing in the ditch on the edge of the road, holding my idol in various broken pieces, bloodstained dreams of true art being wrenched from my sleeve, there was also another reason for my March 27th angst. I'd spent the last seven months shouting in every interview about this artist: "I'm what I am today", "inspirational", "gave birth to me", "my Muse" . . . Christ! This show had better be fucking good. I'd laid my reputation on this; I didn't want society thinking I was born on some cruise ship. You see those doubts arise—maybe last time I was just caught up in the excitement of it all? I was whisky-soaked out of my mind, sleep deprived, blimey! I remember going to see a comedy act in the same week about a man and a giant pen nib and finding it hysterical!

Ladies and gentlemen if you'd like to make your way to your seats . . .

A treasure chest of open stage props awaits your arrival: a circus swing, a mannequin's head sitting upon a grand piano. I see a dress hanging from above. No, two, three, four, many more . . .

"Misery is the river to the world, to the world / Misery is the river to the world," whispers Camille in white face paint. Her delivery of Tom Waits' wonderful piece of work holds the Bloomsbury Theatre mesmerised. This song makes its appearance about halfway through the show. How the hell I got this far without breathing, I'm not sure. You see, Camille doesn't allow you to breath. Like a fucking whirlwind Nigella Lawson feeding Janis Joplin acid cakes. Her work is dirty, is violently fast and holds no shame in pushing breast and arse and intoxicated Rock 'n' Roll nihilism in your face. A winning and memorable combination, but it's when she strips down the band, the cabaret kicks and sparkly shoes, Camille really gets my attention.

This woman can rape an emotion into you with the most beautiful of melodies. Hell, you can be the happiest person on earth and for four minutes you'll find yourself weeping over a lost love you never even had. A clever and dangerous piece of magic to play upon the crowd. Brels Marikie had me breathing backwards. Stunning delivery as she stood barefoot on broken glass (she smashed a wine glass earlier whilst being possessed with Bowie's Moonage daydream). For this musical moment there was no band, no glitz, no glamour—just voice. Captivating. That's what

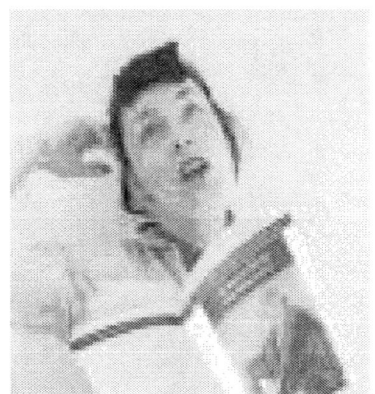

Camille is: she creates a web glistening motionless with intoxicating melodies; her trickery hypnotizes you to gently take refuge in it. The final note fades and you're still bathing in the web. But, oh no! Camille has other plans. She's off with her army of a band behind her, wailing "Brels Next!" And you, my friend, are going nowhere.

So as the evening draws to an end, as we all remain encased in her glistening net, I think to myself, it doesn't really matter if magic lies in trickery or trickery in magic, for she holds the key. And as we all know by Houdini's example, the artist may hold the key but she can't always control the show. That's the beauty of art. She holds the key but we're all being stitched and darned into the web.

As she stepped onto the circus swing for the final song, "Is that All There Is?", a tear rolled down my face. Not for the bitter-sweet irony of the song but for the way I had to look at the gods high above my head where she continued to reign. And it's exhausting chasing from second place, running below unable to take your eyes from above. You smash into things, wounding yourself in fast, violent leaps. Her work is unattainably outstanding. The circus girl will continue to swing high above the air for some time yet—and as for me? Well for as long as she holds the key on the tip of her tongue, I will continue in the hope of that key being passed to my lips, forever chasing and running and stumbling and falling and chasing and running and . . .

'Devotional Doodles' by Patti Plinko

Hobo Poet

by
RC Edrington

This Aint No Punk Rock Song

tattoo stained kids
slam dope inside
porcelain shattered
bathroom stalls

where even rats avoid
hepatitis laced syringes
flicked like
cigarette butts into
a piss soaked corner

& there is no
hip soundtrack bleeding
from a stolen boom-box
to make any of this shit
beautiful or cool

& as for art
no one here
has any use for art
unless he has a $20 bill
& needs his dick sucked

43 Marie

tattoos
blurred like
rubber stamps
on her scarred arms

she pushes
a speed-ball
thru an abscessed

neck vein
to wash a 3 day
heroin coma
from her
tired eyes

eyes that blink
gray to
aquamarine
to yesterday

& her voice soft
like a secret
whispered into
a dead lovers ear
begins to mumble
a story
written with
razorblades
on teenage
wrists

& Marie at 43
becomes simply
Marie at 13
& the ghosts
of drunken fathers
scatter like roaches
from her candlelit
hotel room

as a tear falls
to the cigarette
burnt carpet
& onto a yellowed

photograph torn
from a high school
yearbook

for C.C.

you encouraged me
my art was in language
not subject
so all the bloodstains
& worn syringes
from all the nubile
junkie whores
& quick amphetamine
sex & diseases
scattered thru
my words & syntax
like tarnished pennies
around crisp dollar bills
in that battered guitar case
tossed like a spent body
on that 4th avenue sidewalk
where I used to scream
the blooze
held a value & truth
all their own,
so I scribbled what I knew
& you published
what I knew,
but damn I miss you mama
& learnt enough to know
your name belongs
in one of my jaded
self absorbed pieces
no more than it did
in the obituaries that day
my eyes exploded
with tears like
an infected vein
that shoots pus & blood
against a graffiti scarred
bus depot
bathroom mirror

Live Without A Net: Self-Loathing

**by
RC Edrington**

In absence of windows, I find only mirrors. As shards of fluorescent, fake sunlight slices the darkness and reflects back the emptiness and memory of syringes shattered against a red bricked school yard wall. Perhaps this absence has always been here, yet I failed or chose not to see it through the thin gauze of these tired heroin eyes. Perhaps this emptiness is but another disease I stumbled upon in some unlit alley like a worn $20 bill . . . and now it burns a hole in my pocket as I await the cold, sweaty dreams of the next fix. The fix I pray to some frail, unknown god will never find its way into my limp veins.

    I am not high. I am not numb. Yet I pop 10 pills a day to keep this body sucking air. Diabetes. Heart disease. Mood swings. Depression. They have all taken up residence in this poor excuse of a man who dreams of tomorrows that never come locked inside the four white walls of this 'rehab' facility. In the past few years, I buried my contemporary heroes and friends: Joe Strummer. Dee Dee Ramone. Waylon Jennings. It has gotten to the point where I have more friends dead than alive. Some days I wonder why my corpse was never found among these bodies spent like shell casings in some misunderstood war. Or perhaps I was, and as loser in this macho rock n' roll pissing contest, I was deemed unworthy of notification . . .

. . . in dope rehab they fail to warn of the 30lb bloated circus dwarf that attaches to your stomach almost overnight. A gut that leaves you looking like the cartoon character of your deservedly dead, yet quite innocent alcoholic father. I want to fold myself into myself and disappear like some alien foil found at a UFO crash site in the middle of no-fucking-where New Mexico.

Being clean means I am now free to work meaningless jobs to make cash I can't spend on dope. I am free to fill the empty spaces of my life with the material merchandise that never interested me in the first place. Look mommy, your boy is healthy now. He kicked his dope demon square in the balls. He is now ready to be a good little boy and consume. Here I am America . . . another fuck-up that knows he is a fuck-up and splatters meaningless verse, like blood from a cheap drive-in slasher flick, across the page.

I am at constant search for something of value. Something of substance. Something to fill the absence of the love I found at 19 overdosed on a University street corner in the form of an angel ignored by her makers. Love. How un-cool. Un-hip. Love. Anyone who has been in love and lost it knows every person that follows is just a whore . . . and we pay them in dinners, dates, time or cash. Admit it. We can never be that very first important person in any-one's life again. Not even our own. Something gets sucked out if us and leaves this . . . this . . . absence. And how do you propose we fill that hole?

How am I to live my life if I don't have to walk a tight wire every second of every of minute? I think back to my girls in the hood. The little shorties that peddled their ass every night so their man wouldn't have to wake up sick. I would take a fucking bullet for those girls (and one time did). They had more loyalty and passion for life in one finger than this middle class female creature that stuffs herself daily with TV and Wal-Mart ever will. If you won't die for someone, do you really love them? If you're not out their risking your life everyday, are you really living? Sure, write this all off as hyperbole and bad prose. It doesn't matter anymore than if I wake or fail to wake tomorrow morning. This absence moves slow, cloud-like . . . and you, dearest reader, could be next.

I am not digging on this dope-free life at all. Kicking dope is easy. It's the lifestyle that truly sucks you in and refuses to let go. A lifestyle where each day means everything and nothing at the same single moment. A lifestyle that makes the penning of these very words quite absurd . . .

Jeff Vandemeer – An Interview

1. So tell us about your latest novel, *Shriek*.

I would, but the fungus has spread so far now I can't even read the pages. I don't know if it's my deteriorating eyesight, with the filigree of decay like cracks in the ice of my regard or something to do with the books moldering. Still, if you happen to find a pristine copy and want to pick it up, it's about mushrooms, desperate artists, a deadly hidden secret in the past of the city of Ambergris, and also about the fate of the city's underground inhabitants, the gray caps. Who might be plotting to eliminate humankind, and who might already have created a genocide by 'disappearing' twenty-five thousand people a few hundred years ago. Oh yes, there's also a war going on between two publishing houses and a desperate love affair. Basically, if you like dead Russian novelists but also love H.P. Lovecraft and, er, well, who do you like to read? *Shriek*'s a lot like that author. Or book.

2. It's a film now. What's that all about?

Somewhere inside the half-cracked cranium I call a skull, housing a supposed brain, I thought it might be fun to put together a short film based on scenes from the book, and since I'd always liked The Church and I'd listened to them a lot while writing *Shriek*, I got in touch with them while in Australia, and the rest is history: an art flick that makes *Eraserhead* look normal and that debuted in places like the Clinton Street Theater in Portland, Oregon—and which is now available on the internet.

3. And I hear that somehow you've managed to get *Dilbert* and *Gormenghast* to breed. Can you explain?

In a confluence of disgust and echo-location, I left my day job this past February. The last year there had been one part *American Psycho* and one part *Dilbert*. I just took my personal experiencing, added 50 percent imagination, and wound up with *The Situation*, which will be released as a book from PS Publishing next year. Margo Lanagan and Kevin Brockmeier have both blurbed it. Here's the opening:

My Manager was extremely thin, made of plastic, with paper covering the plastic. They had always hoped, I thought, that one day her heart would start, but her heart remained a dry leaf that drifted in her ribcage, animated to lift and fall only by her breathing. Sometimes, when my Manager was angry, she would become so hot that the paper covering her would ignite, and the plastic beneath would begin to melt. I didn't know what to say in such situations. It seemed best to say nothing and avert my gaze.

4. Margarine or butter?

Butter. It's actually good for you, and not that many calories. We depend too much on artificial stuff in our diets, which is why most of us are either blobs or practically radioactive. Did you know that there are over 300 chemicals found in average households that have never been tested for toxicity? Or that the average diet includes compounds you normally find in stuff you use on your car or for pesticides? So, good old-fashioned butter is fine for me. In fact, just for fun, I've slathered a block of it all over my face while I've been answering these questions. It keeps out the grout.

5. If you could assassinate one political figure in history, hump a second and be a third, which would they be?

That's a dangerous question, given my immediate thought, in the hypothetical. So instead: I think I'd assassinate whoever was responsible for putting the corporations in charge—or slaughter anyone who'd ever had anything to do with making the combustion engine possible. (And don't tell me they're not political!) As for hump, I'm a married man. Even if I went into the past, I think it's retroactive. But, hypothetically, Catherine the Great? I dunno. It is not a question I spend hours obsessing over in my basement office stuffed full of dead animals in formaldehyde jars, the many, many taxidermed frogs, and the old newspapers covering the skeletons of fish who have failed miserably to find roles in my little Real Animal Puppet Theater, which is in the sub-basement under the basement. (I am dismayed that the audience for my art has dwindled to three earthworms, a caged capybara, and the husk of my dead cousin.) As for who I would be if I had my druthers, I would be Saladin, a personal favorite, or I would be whichever Byzantine Emperor was most adroit at staving off the predations of the barbarians, despite having only diplomacy and guile at his disposal.

6. Do you think that counterculture can be popular, or does that defeat the purpose?

I think it's a moot point—the counterculture has been infiltrated by the technology. Now you have people protesting DRM and the fact their damn iPods have restrictions on them. No one's putting their lives on the line for anything other than shopping and holding onto what they have. Even being poor is an affectation for the young, many adopting that lifestyle despite being perfectly capable of working. What we need is a revolution —and the counterculture will be the first against the wall for being hypocritical and for being so self-conscious.

7. Suppose a giant jellyfish descended upon the Earth today and covered the United States. What would you do?

I would probably move to Canada or Australia. I would not like the textural surround-jelly experience of even walking outside to get the newspaper. I've never been fond of jello, living or inert. To live inside of a bubble of it all the time would get tiring. As would the constant raging pain from the stingers.

8. What's the worst thing on TV at the moment?

The worst thing on TV right now is Fox News, followed by all the shows preaching Mega-Materialism so that we can all gorge ourselves on things while the ship goes down.

9. What's your opinion of Darfur?

I am disgusted by our lack of action and our willingness to negotiate with thugs who should quite simply be removed from power. What I find fascinating is we think of genocide as something distant from us, something that could never happen here. Well, it could happen here, and probably will happen here after global warming has destroyed the ability of government to police towns, cities, counties, and states. It's just inevitable, given all the guns.

10. Finally, what does the term New Weird mean to you and how does it differ, if at all, from slipstream?

Slipstream is like a fish that you try to pull out of the river with your hands—it's wriggly and glinty and not at all amenable to your pursuit. New Weird is a building, found in one place, in one context. It is solid and dependable, in that sense, even though what it contains is subversive. Here's the official definition we're using for our anthology from Tachyon. What I find quite interesting is that certain British critics have simply ignored this definition, being unwilling to engage it because their world view is predicated on New Weird being something amorphous, or Something Else. It's fun to see people close their minds and pour cement in their ears.

> *New Weird is a type of urban, secondary-world fiction that subverts the romanticized ideas about place found in traditional fantasy, largely by choosing realistic, complex real-world models as the jumping off point for creation of settings that may combine elements of both science fiction and fantasy. New Weird has a visceral, in-the-moment quality that often uses elements of surreal or transgressive horror for its tone, style, and effects—in combination with the stimulus of influence from New Wave writers or their proxies (including also such forebears as Mervyn Peake and the French/English Decadents). New Weird fictions are acutely aware of the modern world, even if in disguise, but not always overtly political. As part of this awareness of the modern world, New Weird relies for its visionary power on a "surrender to the weird" that isn't, for example, hermetically sealed in a haunted house on the moors or in a cave in Antarctica. The "surrender" (or "belief") of the writer can take many forms, some of them even involving the use of postmodern techniques that do not undermine the surface reality of the text.*

Shriek: An Afterword has been released in a luxurious new limited signed edition by Wyrm Publishing. 500 signed and numbered hardbacks are available for $40.00 each from the Wyrm Publishing store: http://wyrmpublishing.com. Copies include a free soundtrack to the book by The Church.

Agent Apocalypse

by Dave Migman

The city. What can I say? The gutter dog end reality. The trash piling higher and higher, the roads cracking and stinking, shit everywhere, bubblegum, grease, the accumulated spittle frothed from endlessly wagging mouths. The utter bullshit.

Maybe you live in the nice end of town; I don't. I live in a rubbish tip.

The centre city is a different world, the night shows, comedy clubs, nightclubs, pubs, restaurants, chic big windowed bars filled with posers; it all seems like an alien world to me. It may as well be Venus or Saturn. All this strangeness. And who are these people?

Well, they're you.

And here's me—shaking in this horror cell, listening to the show. Radio? TV? No, they are unplugged, as silent as I want them to be. I listen to 'them'—my neighbours.

I try to decipher the words that fuse their world and thus bring this nightly theatre, with timely predictability, seeping through the wall for my benefit: what a lucky guy I am. Yes, every night, from six until twelve their drunken arguments and his football chanting piss stream through a solid brick wall. Both possess that certain resonance, that alcohol-fuelled sonorous ejaculation that is able to pass through half a metre of stone: Constantly rising in tonality; their shouted duets, her solo screaming, crying, grunting moaning, his heartfelt treaties to her battered shadow—YA FUGHING BITCH. GET TAE FUGH YA CUNT. SIT. OBEY. BEND OVER. I especially enjoy the grand finale when he beats her and she pleads as he begins to slap her about and then fuck her against the wall. They deserve each other. Their minds pickled by Buckfast, their intelligence reduced to animal, base, wants, needs, papa takes.

Sometimes I hear him pleading to her, a whining, peevish tone, begging forgiveness/dinner/head. She always caves in, she always consents.

Once in a while he lets off a quiet prayer like a silent fart. He doesn't read, even the tabloid he buys are pictures only. She takes it up every orifice, all for her man, while he lets off a silent prayer that God will forgive him . . . and if you believe the Christian lies, he will.

But I can't stay in here listening to them all the time. What do you take me for? I have work to do. My day job is over; after eight the real work begins.

You see the city is a symptom, the cancerous infection of humanity. So-called civilised . . . and it's dying. Humanity is doomed. I've done the math, I've read the signs enough to realise one thing: THERE IS NO HOPE! The Fall is coming, but it won't be in the fire and brimstone biblical sense. There will be no Rapture. In the end hatred will devour every individual. You only need to look at the children around here to see the signs in the deadness of their eyes, in their hard-man swagger adopted at the tenderest ages. Innocence is wiped away early beneath daddy's drunken scowl; beneath a barrage of fists and verbal abuse; beneath glinting needle eyes, sly smirks. Force-fed gang politics by the age of eight. There is nothing for them to care about.

Why should they? The end is coming and only a fool should believe otherwise.

It is my job to speed things on a little.

There are many different ways of carrying out my chaotic programme. And as much as I would truly love to take a gun and pop them in the street, I must refrain from such crude measures. I do not wish to spend the rest of my time in a cell locked down for twenty-three hours a day.

I hop on the forty-two. I sit upstairs, behind a fat guy who is smoking. I open the window and when he turns I look at him with empty eyes. He turns away, shifting uncomfortably, and I fix my eyes upon the nape of his chubby neck for the remainder of the journey. The bus stinks, alcohol piss and ash. Everything I despise, which is why I sit up there. It helps put me in the mood.

Once in the city I visit the busy burger bars and pubs. I buy nothing but lock myself into a cubicle in their toilets. I remove from my pocket one monster permanent marker and I begin to write "All white girls love black cock" and "White girls are all bitches". In other bars this changes to " Kill the niggers", "Pakis smell of shit", that kind of thing. The message spreads far and wide. The tension grows, the animosity that exists has simply been fuelled once more. Personally I'm not racist. My hatred goes beyond colour and creed; my hatred settles in the very soul of humanity.

Outside as I walk to my next appointment I can almost taste it in the dark streets. I sit on a concrete bench and breathe in the filthy air of the city. It smells like the end. I laugh out loudly into the night.

Next it's to the hospital, where I wait in shadows for the right moment before slipping out and quickly squirting the super hard setting glue into the keyhole of the back door. This trick is best done before they are about to take off, sirens blazing, to scrape up the crushed remains of car casualties from the motorway. Imagine, the paramedics try to leap from the back of the ambulance, time is of the essence, but the door won't budge, the victim starts to haemorrhage . . .

You might say I am an evil man, but that depends upon your conception of right wrong. I believe I'm farsighted. I'm doing you a favour. Look at yourselves—the way you live. The way you are becoming. Divorced from reality. You're all entertainment freaks now. Cathode ray junkies now turning digital broad wave. Society has gone sour; the stench it gives off is repellent, and I'm here to encourage a sweeter change.

Look at yourselves!

I'm in the theatre, watching some Hollywood dross, but before it begins there are at least half-an-hour's worth of adverts, and the people are giggling at them. One of them near me even says, "Oh, that was clever."

It was a fucking advert! I lean forward and tell him if he doesn't shut up I will make him eat his own legs. The couple turn around at me, their faces hanging. He is about to protest, but the sight of my shimmering eyes is enough to silence him. I sit back, unable to hide the large smirk spreading across my face and savouring the sensation and warmth as my cock inches along my inner thigh.

The film is rubbish, but as every one leaves I empty the giblets from the plastic freezer bags into several of the folded seats around me. They glisten in the light of the screen. After this I visit the toilets and write, "All Rangers fans are dirty faggots who suck junky cock" in huge bold letters. I admire my handy work, piss over the seat and leave to visit the cubicles on the lower level to scrawl my anti Celtic nonsense.

Finally the walk back home. I do not take the bus because in every stop along the route, that is twenty-five stops both sides of the road, I plaster little printouts which read: "EVERY DAY YOU DO THE SAME OLD THING. EVERYDAY YOU EAT, SLEEP, SHIT—YOU'RE FUCKED, GIVE IT UP NOW!"

I smile to my self as I do this because I notice the fly-poster removers have had difficulty removing my last "YOU ARE SCUM AND DESERVE EVERYTHING YOU GET! YOU BRING IT ON YOUR-SELVES YOU FUCK-WITS!". I feel quite proud as I make my way back home. The next one I have planned is somewhat shorter. It will read: "STOP BREEDING."

The streets are empty. The only cars are the cold black taxis that race along the glistening roads into the darkness.

Back in my room I set the alarm clock for five. An hour's meditation before my six o'clock electric guitar practice, with the speakers turned towards the neigh-bouring wall and the sound cranked real fucking high.

I lay on my bed in the darkness; I let it fall over me like a blanket.

All in all a pretty successful day, I think.

Emerging
by
Ellen Kombiyil

From the storm cellar to the shock

of exposed air, I noted the house

was gone, but the flamingos
were still standing, albeit with

metal poles twisted at odd
angles, so that their heads—instead

of scanning the horizon, or perhaps
looking at the sky to decide

when to float up and join in the dancing—
were now expressive of various

states of prayer, saying thank you, thank you,
om or amen, repeatedly bowing

in wind, on the verge of dipping
their long beaks into the lake of plenty.

The Beginning
by
Dave Migman

In the beginning the lines went dead. People sat dumb in front of their monitors. Blue screen. Nothing. Just a chill on the shoulders as reality hit home and the heating went off. There was barely a warning, barely a whisper. Some chief economist speculations were skimmed over morning coffees by businessmen waiting flights into the city. No one took such notions seriously. Got to think positive, right?

Then the stocks all fell right out of sight. The great city crash. We stared at our bank notes and used them to wipe our eyes or our arseholes.

A wave of riots on the streets of every city; the televisions went dead; more riots, revolutions and counter strikes; a great plague of human misery as we tumbled back in time. Who let the animals out of the zoos? God only knows.

There can only be great things now. After all the cries have died down and the assassins run out of bullets. There can only be new empires, a new age of hope. The silos remain locked down with their cargoes of purity, but who will work them? The power stations seep radioactive mysteries into vast swathes of land. Our children are twisted out of all human proportion. They are a mutant breed with lives so full, so brief and painful, but they shall inherit a beautiful, pristine earth— where factories sit silent—where crisp packets are lucky finds tacked to great statues of the great sow-faced goddess resurrected from the bog.

God returned, promising his broken children a partial ear. His bitch danced and taught the infant tribes ritual.

This then is the beginning. The great cycle time is lashed to moves once more towards the end.

CONTRIBUTORS

Steve Redwood was born on a rainy day in Britain a long, long time ago. It was still raining twenty-five years later, so he left the country in a huff, a raincoat, and a plane. He is at present hiding out in Madrid.

He has been published in *Talebones, Dream Zone, Enigmatic Tales, Midnight Street, Eureka Literary Magazine, Rhapsoidia*, and even *Quality Women's Fiction,* under the name of a pig-rearing imaginary sister.

Born in Cardiff, **Rhys Hughes** is a prolific short story writer with an eclectic mix of influences, which include Italo Calvino, Milorad Pavić, Jorge Luis Borges, Stanisław Lem, Flann O'Brien, Vladimir Nabokov, Felipe Alfau, Donald Barthelme and Jack Vance. Much of his work is of a humorously eccentric bent, often parodies and pastiches with surreal and absurdist overtones, although he is by no means limited to any of these forms and has proven to be extremely versatile. He has been published in *Postscripts* among many other places, and has authored a number of novels and short story collections, including *The Smell of Telescopes* and *The Percolated Stars.*

Grant Wamack has work that is due to appear in *Twisted Twins: Daily Chills Calendar*.

He lives and dies daily as a student at Northern Illinois University. You can hear him talk about nothing at his blog: http://grantwamack.blogspot.com. If you haven't had enough nothingness you might as well visit him at http://www.myspace.com/gsmooth101.

Steven Archer is an artist and musician living in Baltimore MD. When not recording, DJing, or producing art, he and his wife, author Donna Lynch, tour with their dark electronic rock band Ego Likeness. He has a BFA from the Corcoran School of Art in Washington DC, and has shown his work at galleries and other venues throughout the east coast, and internationally in the form of album art and magazine illustrations.

2008 will see the publication of *Luna Maris,* a book for children which he wrote and illustrated, and Ego Likeness is in the process of recording their fourth album to be released later this year.

PJ Nolan was born in Enniscorthy in the southeast of Ireland in 1966 and now lives with his family near Dún Laoghaire, Co. Dublin.

His poems have appeared in various Irish journals to date, including *West47, Revival* and *The Scaldy Detail* and his chapbook *The Borough* will be launched during the DLR Poetry Now International poetry festival in Dun Laoghaire.

Later this year his poem, *By The Connigar,* will feature alongside those by Eavan Boland, Vona Groarke and Conor O'Callaghan in the US publication *Gender and Geography in Irish Studies* (Cambridge Scholar Press).

Robert Lamb received his B.A. in creative writing from the University of Tennessee and has worked as a high school teacher, journalist, news paper editor and professional writer. He currently lives and works in Atlanta, Ga.

William Doreski teaches writing and literature at Keene State College in New Hampshire (USA). His most recent collection of poetry is *Another Ice Age* (AA Publications, 2007). He has published three critical studies, including *Robert*

Lowell's Shifting Colors. His essays, poetry, and reviews have appeared in many journals, including *Massachusetts Review, Notre Dame Review, The Alembic, New England Quarterly, Harvard Review, Modern Philology, Antioch Review, Natural Bridge*.

Ellen Kombiyil is originally from Syracuse, New York. Her poetry has recently appeared or is forthcoming in 2river, The Dead Mule, Eclectica, MiPOesias, The New Verse News, and Sojourn (UT Dallas), among others. She also had the honor of appearing as Featured Poet for The Hiss Quarterly's April 2007 issue. She currently lives in India with her husband and two children.

Mike Philbin is editor of the Chimericana anthology (now in its fifth year), 3D artist and painter, writer, brainchild behind the subversive writing persona Hertzan Chimera (novels: *Red Hedz, Szmonhfu, Jane's Game*; collections: *Him & Chim & Her, Animal Instincts, BoyFistGirlSuck*). Silverthought Press publish two of Philbin's most recent novels in summer 2008, *Bukkakeworld* and *Planet of the Owls*.

Chet Gottfried thinks the mirror tells him years are passing, but as compensation, publications are increasing. And there's nothing better than having a lovely day in the countryside photographing something beautiful than coming home and writing a twisted story. He keeps telling himself, Write practical. But then the answer is: Twisted is more fun.

Dave Migman is a nomadic type, constantly moving. Currently he lives in Edinburgh but was living in Spain, and before that Glasgow. For a living he carves & engraves stone, which enables him to make money in the summer and get away for the darker months. His writing has been published here and there in the UK over the past five or six years. He also does a lot of artwork/illustration, samples of which you can view here http://migman.blogspot.com.

RC Edrington has been a scourge on the small press for years. His poetry and prose are an ever evolving, brutally honest autobiography. To read more please visit: http://www.rcedrington.com.

Michael R. Colangelo is a writer from Toronto.

Patti Plinko is an artist and performer most noted for being the singer, lyricist and composer of the Dada Noir band 'Patti Plinko & her Boy'.

Micci Oaten is lead singer of the sleaze punk band Paparazzi Whore, who appeared on the BBC's *Singing with the Enemy* last year.

Rosalía Sanfilippo has always been a stubborn ass. While teaching, she published poetry and short stories in college publications and small periodicals. Rosalía continues to publish poetry and short stories in various magazines and journals. Multiple Sclerosis slowed her down a bit, but ultimately it has allowed her to develop in new ways. She now wishes to share her growth and knowledge to help others find their inner mule and kick some ass of their own.

MP Johnson pukes up stories about monsters and weirdoes. He is the mastermind behind Freak Tension fanzine, which focuses on punk rock and things that ear brains. His horror stories have appeared in a range of underground magazines. Find out more about MP Johnson at www.freaktension.com.